PARALYZED
HOPE

STEPHANIE CHRISTIAN

Table of Contents

Chapter One

A yellowish-orange light appears, growing dimmer and then brighter every few seconds. Am I dead? Shifting my head left and right, my eyes struggle to focus on the dancing light. Where am I?

"Sidra, honey?" A feminine voice calls out. A black mass appears in front of me. Blinking a few times, my eyes begin to adjust. "Sidra, honey?" The feminine voice calls out again. Warm hazel eyes greet me. A fuzzy yet familiar face takes shape. "Mom?" eases from my mouth. My vision stabilizes. Large tears roll down her soft brown skin. "Nurse, she's awake!" My mother shouts, disappearing from my view.

Using my elbow, I push myself into a sitting position. A sharp pain shoots to my stomach and up my right arm like an electrical surge. Wincing, I clutch my stomach. Okay, maybe I shouldn't move so fast. Beeps, chattering, and footsteps become loud in my ears.

Two rectangular fluorescent lights illuminate the bland room, giving off a whitish glow. This is exactly where I didn't want to end up, the damn hospital! My heart rate picks up, alerting a heart monitor next to my bed. How do I shut this stupid thing up? Leaning forward, I cover my ears, rocking back and forth. I should be dead.

Radiant light creeps through the window in my room. The stench of bleach rises from the blanket, draping my legs as a few tears drip from my eyes. Cool air flows through the room, drying my damp cheeks. Why didn't I die? I'm so stupid! Why didn't I think about what would happen if my attempt failed? Copious thoughts clouded everything, but in that moment of judgment, I felt free. God, why couldn't you accept my call to come home? I'm tired and sore, inside and out. Why leave me here to suffer with everyone else? Angst scrambles through my body. I swing my legs off the bed; my feet touch the frigid linoleum floor. Adjusting my clinic gown decorated with tiny flowers, I push myself onto my unstable legs. More sharp pain shoots through my right arm. Flinching, I notice the medical tape holding an IV needle steady in my vein. My pills are trash; they couldn't even kill me. I wouldn't be here if they worked in the first place! Picking at the edge of the tape, it begins to peel off bit by bit. Once I get this off, I'm out of here.

"Sidra, what are you doing?" A male voice asks. Letting go of the piece of tape, my head snaps to the door. A tall, slim man strolls towards me. The bit of sunlight sneaking into my room shines on his deep blue eyes. His thick, black, curly hair bounces with each step. I gaze at his nurse scrubs, hugging his caramel-colored body.

"Let's get you back in bed, okay?" the male nurse says with a warm smile. He guides me back onto the stiff bed and covers my legs with the blanket. He grabs a white clipboard with multiple papers attached to it from off the bed frame. Curiosity and anxiety wrestle in my mind while he silently scans through all the papers. Just great; they had to give me such an attractive nurse. I'm here looking like hot garbage while he struts his stuff. His hospital badge sways on the collar of his shirt. Squinting my eyes, I make out the words, *Lake Stone Medical Center Charge Nurse: Bevan Clark.*

"I'm glad you're awake," Bevan says, rummaging through his pockets. "Shoot, I thought I had a pen on me. I'll be right back. Don't try to get up again." I nod. "Also, your doctor will stop by to check on you soon!" He shouts halfway down the hall. In quick shifts, I move my body into a comfortable position. My stomach moans in pain as I lean back against my pillow. I don't regret my choice to end it all. I regret that I didn't choose stronger pills. Footsteps echo up the hall to my room, pulling me out of my head.

"Hello, Sidra, I'm Doctor Wite. How are you feeling today?" He asks, grabbing the clipboard from off the bed.

"I feel okay, but what happened to me?"

"Looks like Bevan hasn't filled out your chart yet." Dr. Wite sighs. Yet again, no one hears me when I speak. I'm so sick of everyone acting like I'm not here. Do I look stupid? Does it look like I have nothing important to say? Then, all of a sudden, they call me a weirdo because I stop talking.

"Let's take your blood pressure real quick." His cold hands wrap the cuff around my left arm. The cuff squeezes harder and harder while he fills out my charts.

"Sidra! I'm so glad you're okay!" my mother shouts, smiling from the doorway.

"Hi," I say, avoiding eye contact. Exhaustion flaunts itself on my mother's face. Dark circles lay around her sunken eyes. She drags an old wooden chair to the edge of my bed. Her stiff legs bend just enough for her body to collapse into the seat.

"Miss Corday, I'm glad you're here," Dr. Wite says, removing the blood pressure cuff from my arm. "How are you doing?"

"It's been a long day," Mom sighs.

"All of Sidra's vitals are fine. The gastric lavage went well, but she will be in some pain. She may experience some nausea for a couple of days. Other than that, she will be fine. You may go when you're ready," Dr. Wite says, placing the chart back on my bed.

"That's wonderful; thank you so much for everything you've done for my Sidra," Mom says.

Wait, it's my body that they poked and grabbed. Why can't Dr. Wite tell me this information to my face? I'm completely invisible. Why do I try anymore? This place is pissing me off. I'm glad we're about to leave. "Feel better, Sidra," Dr. Wite says, walking out of the room. Rolling my eyes, my lips mimic 'Feel Better, Sidra' behind his back.

"We need to tame that wild hair of yours," Mom says with a tired laugh. Dark brown and blonde strands of hair flow down onto her face as she removes the hair tie from her ponytail. She gestures for me to turn my back to her. Facing my back towards her, I wait for her to do what she pleases to my hair. She's probably mad at me; no, she probably hates me. She changed so much in her life to adopt a brat like me. My parents abandoned me when I was 8, so I had to be grown, whatever that was. She saved me, and this is how I repay her, by her finding my almost dead body. A kid like me wasn't worth it; she could have chosen someone better to shower with love. I didn't deserve a new mom. Maybe I should say sorry or something. My mouth opens, but nothing comes out. Words wander around my mouth as my tongue presses against my front teeth. "Mom, are you okay?" I ask. Grabbing my glass from the side table, Mom hands them to me. Slipping them on, I look through the dirty lenses. "Thank you."

She grabs her purse and digs deep down into it. She pulls out a small brush that has bristles going in all different directions. Her gentle, warm hands gather all of my hair in one place. She brushes my hair from the top of my head down to the ends that meet at my shoulders. My hair pulls up and tightens around my head. She twists the rubber band around my hair, making a ponytail. I rub my hands over my hair, pushing down a few stubborn strands sticking out. "Where's my flower clip?" I ask. Mom puts her brush back in her purse and zips it shut. She's never this quiet. Now I know she hates me. My hands grip my gown. "Mom, why won't you talk to me?!" I yell. Tears start forming in the corners of her eyes. My chest tightens; sorrow fills my lungs and surrounds my heart. What kind of daughter am I?

"Mom, please talk to me," I say, looking into her soft eyes. She breaks eye contact with me, "Do you remember anything that happened?" I remember I was trying to kill myself, feeling my lips push out my final words, and everything going black. I can't let her know that I remember; she might get so upset that she abandons me. Then she'd be on the list with everyone who has hurt and left me, and I don't want that for her. She's done too much for me.

"No, I'm sorry, everything is a bit hazy."

She takes a deep breath. "We were out of milk and eggs, so I picked that and some other things up at the store. I came home and called for you to help me with the bags, but you didn't answer back. I dropped the bags at the front door and went to your room. You were lying on the floor unconscious, barely breathing. Your eyes were closed, and tears covered your face. I saw your antidepressant bottle on the floor near your bed. At that moment, I knew," she says, wiping away the few tears escaping from her eyes.

"I called the ambulance; it seemed like forever before they showed up. Holding you close, I cried until they came. They pulled you from my arms, doing everything they could to keep you breathing. You were going to die right in front of me. I couldn't watch," her voice shakes. More tears stream down her face. My stomach aches and groans with guilt. Her pain, it's all my fault. "They put you on the gurney and wheeled you to the ambulance truck while our neighbors stared in confusion. I rode in the ambulance with you to the hospital. I kept asking myself, why would she do this? Am I a bad mother? I prayed to God that he'd save you. I prayed so hard for you, Sidra." Bevan, your nurse, wheeled you down the hall. The doctor told me that they would have to perform an emergency gastric lavage on you."

"What's a gastric lavage? He didn't even explain it to me." What did these people do to me? Her mouth opens up, ready with words. Holding my breath, I prepare myself for an awful answer.

"It's when they pump your stomach, honey."

"Oh," I say, releasing the air in my lungs. Well, that's good to know. I feel less violated now.

"Don't worry, Bevan gave me your flower clip in a small baggy. I'll put it in your hair after you get dressed."

"So, I was brought here this morning?"

"You've been asleep for two days straight." My cheeks grow numb with regret. I put her through so much misery. All I wanted was to be free from mine.

"Sidra, look at me," her voice hardens. My eyes focus on her face. Tears no longer linger in her eyes, only raw pain. "What were you thinking!?" Anger explodes from her mouth. My eyes burn as I try to hold back my tears.

"I'm so sorry; I just wanted to be free!" I shout back. My tongue tingles with fear for shouting at her.

"You telling me sorry doesn't change the fact that you almost killed yourself! You are selfish! Did you think about all the people you'd leave behind? That grief that you want to be 'free' from lands on the people who love you!" she yells.

"I swear all the pens are hiding from me today. I had to search all around the hospital," Bevan says. My hands cover my face. Please, I want to disappear. I can't handle this. I never wanted it to turn out this way. Why did I have to survive?

"Oh... I'm sorry. I can come back later," Bevan says.

"No, no, it's okay. We were talking some things out," Mom says, getting up from the old wooden chair. "I'll be over by the window enjoying the view." She walks towards the window and rests her elbows on the windowsill. "Jesus, thank you for saving my baby girl," she says under her breath, barely audible.

Bevan approaches me, holding a red tray. He places it on my lap. "I bet you're super thirsty," he says. My dry tongue licks at my chapped, sore lips. Giving a quick nod, I look down. A small carton with a picture of a glossy red apple sits on the tray. "It's apple juice. Go ahead, drink up. You need to put something in your body," he says, taking the juice from off the tray. His large hands open the carton up enough for the liquid to flow out freely. Eagerly, I reach for the juice. He places the carton in the palm of my hand, wrapping my fingers around it. The opening touches against my rough lips. I sip the sweet, tangy liquid, letting it moisten my irritated throat.

"Is it good?" he asks, taking the tray off my lap.

"Yes, it's very good; apple juice is my favorite."

"Miss Corday, your guests are here," Bevan says. She turns from the window, flashing us both a grin,

"I'll be right back," she says, walking out of the room.

Guests? Who would come and visit me while I'm like this? I don't have any friends. Maybe it's family? No, it couldn't be. I doubt they know anything about this yet.

"Are you done with your juice?" Bevan asks, reaching for the carton.

"Oh yeah, thanks. Can I please have another one?"

"Sure, I'll get you a few more when the guests come in. I don't want to be in the way."

I'm so excited to go home. It's already been a long day, even though I just woke up. I'm sick of looking at these plain white walls. I'll have a nice hot bubble bath and forget this whole mess ever happened.

Chapter Two

My mother's laughter and unknown voices flood the hall. Tilting to my left, I look at the doorway. My mom walks into the room alone. She pulls two more chairs up to my bed. Shallow breaths leave my mouth in rapid succession, and my chest begins to ache. My nervous lungs trap what little air I have left in my body. Swallowing hard, I prepare myself for the mysterious guests to enter the room. Come on, keep it together, they know Mom, so they should be nice.

An average-looking woman I've never met before makes her way to one of the chairs. She sits down and smiles at me with coffee-stained teeth. Who the heck is this chick? Maybe she works in the hospital. The woman yanks her pink shirt down over the top of her jeans. She shoves her blonde hair away from her rosy cheeks. Her eyes lock onto mine.

"Hey, Sidra, I'm Rayna," she extends her hand out towards me. Her smile expands as we shake hands. Sweat from her palm releases us from the formal greeting. Using the edge of my gown, I wipe the remaining sweat from my hand. A large man with swept-back hair stands next to the window, talking to Mom.

"Who's the huge dude that you brought with you?" I ask. Rayna pulls out a tan-colored folder from her business-savvy purse.

"The 'dudes' name is Cynric. He's my partner, sort of like a bodyguard. He ensures my safety as well as the clients. You can meet him later if you want." What would he be protecting me from? He looks in my direction, my reflection distorts in his dark sunglasses. My chest tightens.

Bold black letters sit across the top of the folder Rayna placed on the bed. *P.E.R.T. Cases.*

"What's P.E.R.T.?" I ask, raising an eyebrow. She opens the folder up,

"P.E.R.T. is short for Psychiatric Emergency Response Team," she says, shuffling through the papers. She pulls out a sheet with my name and other information scribbled on the top. *Sidra Corday: Case number 1017.* That's not cool; they have my information and didn't even ask for my permission. Isn't that against the law or something?

"Why are you here? I don't see an emergency. As a matter of fact, I'm about to go home."

"We specialize in helping people with suicidal ideations. We help them become safe and stable again," Rayna says with pride.

"Okay, good for you guys, but I don't need any help, but thanks. You guys can leave now."

"Sidra, you tried to take your life by overdosing on your antidepressant, am I right?"

"So what? I'm better now," I snap.

Rayna's face exposes her distrust in me. "I'm glad that you feel better now, but it doesn't erase the fact that you sought out suicide. You have some underlying mental health issues that need to be addressed. We don't want this to happen again." Would I try again if another chance appeared? I can't even answer that myself. She can't know that, though.

My lips curl and curve, attempting to become a smile. "Trust me, I'll never try to kill myself again," I say, still forcing a smile. Rayna's face softens. This is wasting my time. I don't need any help. I wouldn't be in this situation if my actual psychiatrist had helped me the first time.

"Look at your mother. Put yourself in her shoes. Wouldn't you be heartbroken if you found your daughter on the floor, half dead? If I let you go because you smiled sweetly at me, I wouldn't be doing my job right. I'd be doing a disservice to you, your mother, and everyone else who cares about you. Quick question Sidra, are you okay with leaving your mother behind with such an awful heartbreak and crippling guilt?"

"No, but-"

"I didn't think so," she cuts in.

"Every day, I meet people who crave death as a release for their trauma. I hear the same things several times a day. Promises of how they'd never try again are number one on that list. Some truly mean it, but others will try again as soon as you turn your head. I can't leave here today, giving you the responsibility of handling your mental health alone. Your blood would be all over my hands. Do you understand?" Rayna asks. Mom and Cynric nod to every word flooding from Rayna's mouth. Okay, let's say I agree to this crap, how would they help me? Will they come home with me and watch me like hawks for a few days, then leave? I wouldn't mind, I guess, as long as I get to go home.

Cynric removes his flip phone from his shirt pocket and checks a text message. "Rayna, we have to wrap this up. We have another case that's come up," he says.

"Alright, Sidra, here is where your Mother, Cynric, and I stand. We think it would be best if we admit you into a psychiatric hospital," she says.

"You're joking, right? I ask, looking at them.

Rayna shakes her head.

There's no way I'm going! They can't force me to go! I may have just turned 18, but I have a say now. What if they hurt me in there? What if they keep me in there forever? Why would my mother allow this? They must have tricked her. If they want to force me, they'll have to find me. There's no way in hell I'm going without a fight. Sweltering rage pulses through my body as my fist clenches.

"Yeah, please hurry; we have another case after this," Cynric says to someone over the phone.

Who's Cynric talking to? He must be calling the cops. He's going to make them handcuff me. They're going to drag me away forever! "I'm not crazy! You can't force me to go!" I yell at Rayna. Fear and concern take over her face as she gets up from the chair. She makes her way over to Cynric and whispers into his ear. I need to leave before they cage me up like an animal.

Shifting my weight towards the edge of the bed, I force myself onto my feet. "Sidra, why are you getting out of bed?" Rayna asks. They can't take me.

Tears spill from my eyes. Bolting out of the room and down the hall, my lungs fight for air. Loud, startling footsteps come from behind me. "Sidra, stop!" Cynric commands. Crap, of course, Rayna would send him to catch me.

Pressing faster, my gown flaps against my body. My glasses become blurry with tears. Frightened nurses, doctors, and patients jump out of the way. "Someone stop that young lady, please!" Cynric's voice booms down the hall.

A nurse in black scrubs takes his position towards the end of the hall. Spreading his legs, his arms open wide. Do you think that's going to stop me?! Rage shoots to my feet. My shoulder rams into the nurse's chest. His back smacks against the wall, knocking the wind out of him. Looking behind me, several doctors flock to aid the man. Maybe I was too rough. Whatever, I need to worry about myself right now.

Navigating through the hospital, I sprint around several more corners. My chest expands and releases harsh, heavy breaths. Slowing down, I begin to jog. I'm so lost. Where are the exits in this place?

Turning around another corner, teal double doors catch my attention. Please be the way out. Pressing my hands against the hefty doors, I push them open.

Large, circular lights hang from the ceiling, illuminating a black, plastic-looking hospital mattress. Long white, black, yellow, and blue cords dangle from several machines. A screen with a white frame hangs above the machines, showing everything in the room, including me. This must be an operating room. It feels like I'm just going further into the hospital, great.

Leaning my back against the wall, I slide down, letting my butt sit on the floor. Anxiety ascends up my back, wrapping itself around my spine. Pulling my knees to my chest, I tug on the hem of my gown, trying to cover my legs.

Why can't they understand my side of things? It isn't fair. Rayna and Cynric don't know what it's like to be abandoned. They never had to deal with being damaged physically and emotionally by family members. Maybe if they knew my true struggle, they too would seek freedom. My body relaxes as I close my eyes.

Uneven footsteps come down the hall; they pause, then proceed, then pause again. My eyes pop open. How did they find me already? If it's Cynric, I'm ready to put up a fight. I don't care how intimidating he is. Squeezing my gown, I brace myself for the worst.

Chapter Three

The double doors swing open. "Sidra, it's me, Bevan. Are you in here?" he whispers. Bevan's head peeks around the door. "There you are. May I sit with you?" I nod. Sitting down next to me, he crosses his long legs.

"Everyone is looking for you."

"I know, but that's because they're trying to send me to a psychiatric hospital."

"Oh, I see. You had me worried. I had to sneak away to come find you."

"Not to be rude or anything, but why are you going the extra mile for me?"

He looks at me and chuckles. "Welp, looks like it's story time." His face shifts from a happy glow to a face with sorrow-filled eyes. "Back in high school, I knew this guy. His name was Zax. We had many classes together, and he also lived on the same street as me. We eventually started talking and got to know each other bit by bit. We weren't like best friends, but it was nice to talk and joke around with him. We'd walk home from school together a lot. Sometimes, we would be laughing, and then silence would take over. At those moments, he'd share some things with me."

"What kind of things?" I ask, leaning forward for more.

"He'd say stuff like, 'Would you rather have family hurt you or a complete stranger? Cause I'd choose a stranger every time.' So I started thinking, maybe he's struggling with family issues. I didn't know what to say when he started talking like that. I'd usually nod and pat him on the back." Bevan glances up at the ceiling and clears his throat.

"One day at school during lunch, he came up to me; he looked like he had been crying. He looked me dead in the eyes and said, 'I wish I could run away, so far away that I'd run off the edge of the earth.' At that moment, I was confused, and I didn't know what to say. So, I said the first thought that came to mind, 'It's okay, buddy, just cheer up.' He looked at me as if I didn't respond. When school was over, I saw him already down the street, walking home. I assumed he wanted to be alone, so I lingered at school for a while, then went home."

"Long story short, Sidra, I went to school the next day. The halls were loud with chatter, louder than ever before. The students and teachers were all talking about Zax. Word went around that Zax ran away in the middle of the night to Cobble, the next town over. He jumped off their newly built bridge and died. I felt so guilty because it felt like it was my fault, but I didn't know why at the time. I knew he was acting weird, but I couldn't say anything right to make him feel better. So, I promised myself to always try to help when someone is trying to confide in me, whether I fully know what they are going through or not. You, Sidra, were my reminder. You must be hurting so bad to put yourself through that," he says. Tilting his head back up to the ceiling, he tries to hide the feelings leaking from his eyes. Just like Bevan, I'm not sure what to say to people who are hurting right in front of me. Saying something in these situations always feels like I'm defusing a bomb. I'd want to cut my tongue out if I said something that'd make their situation worse. He clears his throat again.

"Anyways, why are you against going to a psychiatric hospital?" He asks.

"I've never been to one of those places before. It sounds scary. What will my family think about me after they hear about this? I don't want to be labeled crazy for being admitted."

"I know it sounds scary, but you need this. They can really help you there. Who knows, maybe you'll meet some nice people."

"How do you know? How can I believe you?"

Bevan raises his pinkie finger in the air, "I pinkie promise, if anything happens to you, they will have to deal with me and your mom. Besides, why would your mom risk putting you in a place that's not meant to help you? So, what do you say? Do you trust me?"

At this point, I've got nothing to lose if he's wrong. I'll be forced to go if I'm here or in a holding cell for running. Here's to hoping he knows what he's talking about. My pinkie finger clings around his. Warmth floods my cheeks as I smile. "If anything happens, then you'd have to deal with my mom too," I say with a giggle.

Bevan glances down at my arm and lets go of my pinkie. "You're bleeding," he says, pulling my right arm closer to his chest. He twists and turns, examining my forearm and wrist. "I should be wearing gloves for this," he mumbles.

"How am I bleeding? I don't think I hurt myself; I don't feel any pain," I say, looking down at the trail of dry blood that's made its way down to my wrist.

"The IV must have ripped out when you ran out of the room, I'm guessing. Most people forget they still have a needle in their arm when they are discharged and move too fast, hurting themselves. Let's head back so I can clean it up and bandage it for you," he says, getting up with ease.

"Ready to go?" Pushing off the wall, I prop myself up onto my shaky legs. "Let me help you." Locking my fingers in between his, I straighten my body out. His eyes connect with mine.

"Sorry about worrying you. The only thing on my mind was survival. I haven't had to depend on that since I was little," I say. He pushes the doors open, leading me out as he clasps his fingers between mine even tighter.

"I want you to live your life to the fullest; I think God has something planned for you," he says, looking straight ahead. God? Why would he use someone like me? It's like using a broken pot to hold precious water. It's useless.

Our footsteps sync and create a soothing rhythm as we walk down the empty hall.

"Um, Bevan,"

"Yes?"

"If you see a male nurse wearing black scrubs who looks injured, can you please tell him I'm so sorry? I didn't mean to hurt him like that."

"Don't worry, I'm sure he knows you weren't trying to hurt him intentionally. I'll give him your apology," he says, grinning.

"Why are you smiling like that? It's kind of creepy."

"Because you have a soft heart underneath all that worn-out armor." Being soft only leads to more pain.

"Guess what? We have arrived at your room. Don't be afraid. I believe you'll help so many people. Your journey will start today." Placing his large hands against my back, he pushes me into the room little by little. "I'll be back with your juice and bandages for your arm," he says, walking down the hall.

Apprehension drifts through the room as Cynric, Rayna, and my mom stare at me. What do I say? Cynric and Rayna look pretty pissed off.

"Hey guys, how's it going?" Cynric's muscular arms flex as he makes his way over to me.

"Don't run from us; if you try that again, I'll have the staff at the hospital keep watch of you 24/7. You won't be able to breathe without their permission," he yells. His hair droops over onto his forehead. Dude looks like he ran a marathon, even though it was only through a few halls; how is he out of shape when he has arms like that? A small giggle slips past my lips.

"What's so funny? Do you want your stay there to be miserable?"

"No, I'm sorry, I tried to run. It won't happen again," I say as sincerely as possible. Since I'm already going, I don't want to make it even worse for myself. His sweaty face softens like room-temperature butter. "I'm glad you have come to your senses," he says, slicking back the drooping hair from off of his forehead.

"The ambulance will be here in twenty minutes to take you there," Rayna says.

"Do I have to wear this gown?" I ask.

"No, I went home to pack your clothes for you last night. I've put everything you'll need inside the bag. This was planned after we found out that you'd be okay," my mom says from across the bed.

"Okay, I'm ready to get out of this ugly gown." Mom crouches down next to the side of the bed. She bounces back up like a spring. She places a purple medium-sized duffle bag in the middle of the bed.

"Thanks. Can I have a little privacy now to get changed?" I ask, placing my hands on my hips. Suspicion circulates as they stare at me.

"I told you I won't run again."

"Okay, we'll just be right outside this door. Remember what Cynric told you if you feel the itch to run again," Rayna says. Cynric, Rayna, and my mom exit the room, and the door closes behind them.

Removing my hospital gown, I let it fall to my feet. My black pants and green T-shirt greet me as I open the duffle bag. I put on my shirt and pants. Pulling my old sneakers from the bag, I shove my feet into them. The dry blood on my forearm causes my skin to itch. Ugh, I feel nasty. I need a shower.

"Sidra, are you done getting dressed?" my mom asks from outside the door. "Yeah," I shout. The door opens. "You look nice," Rayna says with a plastered smile on her face.

"Hey, I'm back," Bevan says, pushing the door further open with the side of his foot. He places another red tray down on the bed. "Come sit next to the tray so I can fix up your arm." I sit on the edge of the bed, holding my arm out to him. He slides on a pair of blue latex gloves and opens up a small packet of alcohol wipes. He grips my arm with one hand, cleaning up the blood with the other.

A few cartons of apple juice, now accompanied by bendy straws, sit on the tray. My lips quiver, craving for its sweetness to surround my tongue again.

"You're all patched up."

"Thanks, I was getting tired of seeing the blood." Plucking the apple juice from the tray, I sip from the straw, savoring the taste.

Loud, irritating beeps come from Rayna's purse hanging off the edge of the wooden chair. "Sorry, I'll see who that is," she reaches for her phone, which is squeezed into a little pocket on the side of her purse. "The ambulance is outside waiting; get your stuff, Sidra," Rayna says, leaving with Cynric.

Bevan looks at me and nods. I wish I didn't have to go, but I made a promise. He unfolds a wheelchair from the corner of the room. He gestures for me to sit down. If I do this and come out alive, maybe Mom will be happy with me again. Grabbing my duffle bag, I sit in the wheelchair.

"Are you still scared?"

"Yes, but I'm ready to give it a try."

The wheelchair glides across the smooth floor, feathery breeze tickles my cheeks as we travel down the hall. "When you come back to Lake Stone, tell me everything, the good and the bad. I know you will meet people your age and see that you are not alone in this fight." I nod.

Two glass doors slide open, letting the golden rays of the sun shine down on my skin. It's amazing how you can forget how wonderful the outside feels. Out in the distance, my mom waves her arm next to the ambulance truck. I guess Rayna and Cynric left already; it must have been something super serious.

Red and blue stripes stretch from the front of the truck to the back. Two sets of red and white lights at the top of each corner of the truck reflect a mild glow from the sun. Blue, thick letters shimmer against the white paint, reading Lake Stone Emergency Ambulance Unit.

The seat of the wheelchair wobbles up and down as the wheels roll over the parking lot's gravelly asphalt. Bevan parks the wheelchair in front of my mom.

"Thank you so much, Bevan, for everything you've done," she says, reaching out her arms to him.

"It was a pleasure helping you guys. We'll meet again very soon," he says, hugging her.

"Let's get you out of this chair," he says as he squats down to my feet, raising both of the metal footrests. His hand rests on my knee as he looks into my eyes, "I'm so proud of you for being so brave. Remember, when this is all done, you will tell me everything."

"I wouldn't have been able to do this without you. I'll tell you every detail when I get back," I say, smiling. He takes my hand and helps me out of the wheelchair and onto my feet. He wraps his arms around me tightly.

"I better get back now; it's starting to get busy. Good luck, Sidra," he says, letting go of me. Bevan pushes the wheelchair across the parking lot and back into the hospital.

"Sidra, I have something for you," my mom says.

"What is it?" I ask. She digs through her purse and pulls out a clear baggie.

"Turn to your left for me." Turning to my left, I face the green trees rustling in the crisp wind. Her hand touches the side of my head.

"I'm putting your clip in your hair," she pushes down, letting the clip snap into place.

"Thank you, I wouldn't have been able to go without it," I say.

"I was saving it for this moment. I'm going to miss you, please know that I'm coming back for you. I'm not going to leave you there. I know you will get better. Please use this time wisely." Hugging her, I smell her sweet perfume. Her arms hold me against her body as she rubs my head.

"Hi, um, are you Si...Sidra? Did I pronounce your name right?" A tall, athletic woman holding a very thick metal clipboard approaches me. She points to her right shoulder, showing her paramedic badge on her dark blue uniform.

"Yeah, you said my name right," I say, looking at her eyes, draped in black eyeliner and mascara.

"My name is Iona. I'm here to take you to Pleasant Horizons Psychiatric Hospital."

"I will see you soon, I guess," I say, letting go of my mom.

"You are going to have to lay on this gurney," Iona says, pulling out the gurney from the back of the truck. The bright yellow poles unfold, releasing the hidden wheels. She wrestles around with it for a short moment until several snaps and pops come from the gurney. The wheels fully extend and make contact with the asphalt.

Iona takes my duffle bag from the ground. She pats the gurney, inviting me to lay on it. Lying flat on my back, I look up at the clear sky. She pushes the head end of the gurney up, putting me into a sitting position, and places a pillow behind my head. "There you go, you sure do look comfy. I'm going to have to strap you to the gurney to ensure your safety during the ride."

"How long will it take for us to get there?" I ask.

"Well, it is 4 pm right now. I think we will make it there at 6 pm," she says, flopping two long black straps over my stomach, lower arms, and legs. Two long hours of being strapped to a bed with wheels. This is already so much fun. Do they think I'd freak out and jump out of the moving truck? Maybe someone tried, and they didn't want that to happen again.

She pushes the straps into two metal buckles and, pulling tight, she secures them. She lifts and pushes me into the truck, making the gurney lock into place. Hopping into the truck, she sits next to me on a little bench.

"Ready, Iona?" A deep voice asks from the front of the truck.

"Yes, sir, " she says, pulling hard and slamming both doors shut.

"Let's go!" she shouts to the front. The engine roars and rumbles. My body jiggles on the gurney as I feel the truck start to move. Looking out the small rectangular windows on the metal door, I see my mom waving goodbye. A lump sits in my throat, and reality begins to smother me.

"Are you nervous?" I nod. "It'll be alright, by the way, I love your hair clip. I wish we could accessorize when we're on duty," she says. The motion of the truck rocks me, soothing my body. My eyelids become heavy as they struggle to stay open. Iona's voice fades away as she drones on about makeup and fashion. My eyes close.

"Sidra, wake up; we're here." My eyes gradually open, and I look around. The truck comes to a complete stop. Iona opens the doors and jumps out. She pulls the gurney out, letting the wheels touch the ground. "What a long ride," she says, stretching her arms.

Grabbing the end of the gurney, she pulls me across the parking lot. She stops a couple of inches away from a black dusty door. A small talk box with a red button is attached to the door frame. Iona presses the red button and steps back. The box lets out a loud, long beep.

"It's Iona from Lake Stone Ambulance with a Sidra Corday," she shouts into the box. A loud buzz comes from the door. She pushes the gurney back, making room for the door to open. She drags me through the doorway, looking behind her until the door closes.

As the gurney swings around the corners, I inhale. It smells like a regular hospital. Are we in the right place? The walls are decorated with colorful paintings of trees, flowers, bees, and butterflies. I'm so confused. Am I in a daycare facility? This isn't what I imagined it would look like. The gurney stops in front of two large, thick glass windows separated by a slither of black rubber. Iona taps against the glass hard with her metal clipboard.

A lady with copper-red hair appears in the window. She slides it open.

"This is Sidra Corday, right?" she asks, her voice hoarse.

"Yeah, can you sign this while I unbuckle her?" Iona asks, handing her the metal clipboard through the window.

"Alright, time to get off; I know it's comfy," she smiles, lowering the gurney to her feet. She presses the buttons, letting the metal buckles release the straps. They fall to the side of the gurney, slamming against the floor, creating an echo around us. My joints crack and pop while I stretch. It feels so good to be able to move again. I push myself onto my feet.

"Don't forget your bag," Iona says, reaching around to the back of the gurney, pulling out my duffle bag.

"Thank you," I say, taking the bag from her hand.

"Sidra, sit in that chair," the red-haired nurse says, pointing to a plastic white chair against the wall. Sitting down, I watch Iona lift the gurney back up.

"Good luck, Sidra," she says, taking her clipboard back from the nurse. She rolls the gurney down the hall, disappearing around the corner.

"A nurse will be right out to check you in, alright, Sidra," the red-haired nurse says.

"Okay, thank you," I say. She slides the glass window to the right, closing and locking it.

A couple of patients walk into a medium-sized room. They wander around looking lost. A long hall to my right has several doors on both sides. Well, at least the hospital seems nice. This won't be so bad, I've got this, I hope.

Chapter Four

Tuesday, Day 1

“Sidra Corday, please follow me.” A squat lady wearing faded blue nurse scrubs stares at me. Her short, brown hair hugs her tan face.

“Hello, can you hear?”

“What? Sorry, I’m kind of tired,” I say, staring into her uninterested eyes.

“I bet you were too busy running around the hospital. Hurry up, I have other things to do,” she says, turning around. Wow, Cynric must have already blabbed about my little adventure earlier. Maybe he called ahead so they could keep me in line, figures. She walks down the hall and makes a sudden left turn. The hot pink lanyard around her neck holding multiple keys jingles as she walks. Following her, I peek around the corner.

She shifts through all the keys on the lanyard, looking for the proper one. Unlocking it, she swings open the heavy door.

“Before we go in, I’ll need your bag. Another nurse will take you to log in your personal belongings later. Wait here,” she says, taking my bag from my hands. Shoving my hands into my pants pockets, I peek into the small room. Everything seems okay so far, except for the bitter nurse.

"I left your bag in the nurse's area. That's the area behind the big glass window, if you didn't already know," she says, rolling her eyes. She walks into the room and sits down at a large wooden desk. "What are you waiting for? Sit down. I don't need to hold your hand like a little kid, do I? Close the door behind you." Making sure the door closes behind me, I take my seat across from the nurse.

She scans through several folders and slides pieces of paper out from them. Behind her head, a medium-sized poster hangs against the dull white wall. *We Are Your Helping Hands* is sprawled out across the poster in glittery purple letters. Poorly drawn hands of different colors are scattered all around the words. Swirling her desk chair around, she faces me.

"I'm Katrina. I'm one of the underpaid staff that works here. My job is to look after patients like you daily," she says, looking at me with a stale expression.

"Date of birth?"

"Um, October 4th, 1989." She scribbles on the sheet of paper.

"So, how'd you get the invitation to stay at Pleasant Horizons?" She asks.

"I tried to kill myself," I mumble

"Uh, can you speak a little louder?"

"I tried to kill myself!" I holler.

Katrina smirks and writes on her paper.

"Between you and me, why would you want your life to end? You're so young," she says.

"Look, I don't want to talk about it."

"Ha, that's a good one. Well, guess what? You'll have to share what's inside, whether you like it or not. There are several meetings every day, made just for you. They make you talk about your feelings and all the delightful things that people love to hide," she says with wide eyes and a twisted grin.

"Something else you should know: all the meetings are mandatory. If you skip any sessions, that tells us you need to stay longer to get better."

Sorry, I didn't know this was a prison. Wouldn't forcing patients to talk about hard things make their mental health worse? Since it's mandatory, I'll show up, but no one can make me talk. They'd have to pry my mouth open with their bare hands.

"What if I don't feel well and have to miss one?"

"Good question. Make sure you tell one of the staff members around here. But don't go thinking that you can use that excuse more than once," she says, laughing a little under her breath.

"Katrina! Katrina!" A voice shouts from the other side of the metal door. "I know you're in there!"

"I recognize that voice," she mumbles as she gets up from her chair. She opens the door a bit and pokes her head out. The door swings open, pushing her back and out of the way.

"Axel, how many times have I told you not to interrupt staff when they are checking in new patients?" She asks, crossing her arms over her chest. Trying to sneak a look, I slide forward in the chair. Who's Axel?

"The staff here are awful. You've even said it yourself," the young man blurts out.

She rolls her eyes, "What did you do now?"

"I didn't do anything. It's all his fault!" He shouts.

She sighs, "Okay, stop yelling; I have a patient in here. You're probably scaring her. Calm down and tell me what has you so upset?" He steps into the room and leans his butt against the desk. His green and white striped hoodie hangs loose on his slim body.

"I've been waiting for an hour for my towels. I need to take a shower now," he says.

"Axel, you know you have to ask for towels," Katrina says.

"You don't think I know that? I've asked him over and over, and he says the same thing, 'Give me a minute, I'll get it.' It's been an hour! He likes all the other patients except for me, I'm telling you!" He shouts.

He lets out a long sigh while running his fingers through his short Mohawk. The left and right sides of his head are shaved down. The intense black from his hair complements his ivory skin.

"How about this? I'll get your towels, but let me finish checking her in. You know you can trust me; I'm your favorite nurse here," she says with a sweet smile. Axel lets out a wild laugh.

"Don't flatter yourself so much, Katrina," he says, smirking.

This guy is annoying and self-absorbed. He sounds like he runs this place. I wonder if he makes the others bow down to him. King Axel. Looking at his full pink lips create word after word. I let out a heavy sigh. Even though he is pretty annoying, I can't stop looking at him. He's just so loud and over-dramatic. He turns to me, "Can I help you with something? Do you have a staring problem?" He asks. His beautiful pearl-gray eyes lock onto mine. I've never seen anyone with that eye color before. They're amazing. My mouth opens in awe.

"Hello!?" he shouts. His harsh, loud voice snaps my gaze from his rare eyes.

"First of all, you don't have to be rude; I was looking at that poster over there," I say, hiding my embarrassment.

He turns away from me and back at Katrina. "I'll be in my room; please bring my towels," Axel says, walking out.

"You're lucky that I care, you little brat!" She shouts, leaning out the doorway. Her voice echoes down the hall.

"Yeah, Yeah!" He shouts back.

Katrina closes the door and massages the sides of her head. She sits back down at the desk. "I swear that boy is making me age like crazy," she grumbles.

"Sorry for the interruption. Let's get back to checking you in." A few of her fingers tap rapidly on the desk.

"Do you take any antidepressants?"

"Yes, but I don't remember the name of them, sorry," I say, thinking about the blue round tablets filling my mouth.

"It's fine, we'll worry about that later. What's your mother's name?"

"Tara Corday," I say as I watch her scribble my mother's name down.

"Does your family suffer from a history of mental health issues?"

"I'm not sure, to be honest. I'm adopted, so I don't know much about my biological family," I say, twiddling my thumbs.

Just speaking about my parents puts me in a bad mood. They're the last thing I want to think about. My plate is already full with a bunch of crap that I don't want to deal with. She rubs her face with both of her hands, her eyes looking overworked but still uninterested.

"Do you have any medical conditions?"

"No."

"Is this your first time being admitted to a psychiatric hospital?"

"Yes."

"Good, because I never want to see you back here again. Okay, we have a few more questions."

I smile, feeling relieved.

"Do you smoke, drink, do drugs, and are sexually active?"

"No, I don't smoke, drink, or do drugs," I hold my tongue, struggling to find the words to say. Why does she need to know the answer to the last question? My cheeks become warm from the thought.

"I don't have to tell you that," I declare.

"Ha, relax, you don't have to answer it. It's always fun asking new patients to see them squirm around in their seats. It gives me a good laugh each time," she says with a big grin.

Rolling my eyes, I look back down at my thumbs. "Don't look at me like that. You'd better get used to intrusive questions. Nothing is kept a secret here, and it's best not to fight it." What's her damage? I guess when you work here long enough, you would rather torture your patients than help them. She was kind to Axel, though, which is weird because he's a jerk.

"Anyways, the psychiatrist that's assigned to your case only comes in on Thursdays. You have a full day to get situated, seeing that it's only Tuesday," she says. I nod.

"All the questions are out of the way. It's time for the part that everyone loves!" She shouts with excitement.

"Time to take a look at what kind of crazy things you've done to your body. Also, to see if you're smuggling contraband between your butt cheeks," she says, laughing.

"You're just messing with me again, right?"

"Nope, please stand up. Spread your legs and hold out your arms."

Standing up, I spread my legs and hold out my arms. Katrina stretches blue latex gloves over her small hands. She pats around my chest, waist, and legs. She digs two fingers around my shoes and into my socks. Feeling around my butt, she digs into all the pockets of my pants.

"Looks like you're clean. I'm glad because I was not in the mood to get stabbed in the face today."

"Are we done now?" I ask, feeling violated.

"Nope, not yet. I need to examine your body for any scars, cuts, or bruises. Take off your clothes now," she says with a serious look on her face. Cool, this just got worse. She better not ask me to bend over and cough twice for her.

"You can keep your undergarments on," she says, adjusting her gloves on her hands. Complaining under my breath, I remove my shirt and pants. Looking up at the ceiling, I pray that we don't accidentally share eye contact. She pulls an outline of a human body from one of the folders on the wooden desk. She assesses my body.

"Hmm, lift your left arm. I thought I saw something." I lift my left arm. "So you're one of those people. You like to take your anger and sadness out on yourself by performing self-mutilation," she says, looking disappointed.

"I did, but I stopped. I'm proud because it was hard, but I got through it; that's why I'm at ease with my scars." Katrina smiles and nods.

"You can put your clothes back on now," she says, writing my name on the human outline sheet. She draws several horizontal lines on the left arm of the human outline.

"Would you like me to remove your hospital band and bandage for you?"

"Yeah, sure." She pulls the bandage off my arm in a swift motion, leaving a burning sensation behind. Then she takes the hospital band and snaps it off my wrist with her hands.

"Can you sign here stating that we told you about our confidential policies?" She asks as she hands me the pen. I take the pen from her soft hand and sign my name next to the big X.

"Before I can let you go, I need you to remove your laces from your sneakers."

"Why do I need to remove my shoelaces?"

She gathers all the papers off the desk with one big swoop. "You can strangle yourself to death with shoelaces. People come up with pretty unique ways to try to kill themselves in here. We have to be extra safe, even if it does sound ridiculous."

In a zigzag order, I pull out my old, dirty laces from my shoes and hand them to her. "Finally, we're done!" She shouts, raising her hands in the air. "Your laces will be held in the nurse's area until you're discharged." I nod and stand behind her as she opens the door.

"Wait, Um, Katrina?"

"Yes, what is it?" She turns around.

"How long were we in there?" I ask. She looks down at her small red watch. "We were in there for about an hour and 10 minutes."

"Thanks, you've made this experience very strange," I say with a smile.

"I do my job well. You can sit in the hall chair by the nurse's window or go into the meeting room and mingle with the others.

It's your call, but a nurse by the name of Finch will be with you soon to log in all your personal items," she says, her face softens.

I wonder if she only wears that mask during check-in; she does a good job hiding her feelings; I should know.

"Thanks," I say, watching her walk down the lengthy hall.

"Axel, come get your towels!" She yells.

Walking to the meeting room window, I look through the glass littered with greasy fingerprints. Three people sit around a plastic white table, flinging flimsy playing cards at each other.

Next to them, a big black TV rests in a case. A thick transparent plastic sheet covers the front of the case, locking the TV inside. Scratch marks and graffiti signs are etched all around the borders of the specially molded covering. The people who work here are so paranoid. There's no reason to lock a TV up like that. Unless someone wanted to throw the TV at someone in a blind rage, anything can happen, I guess.

My feet drag along the floor as my sneakers flop on and off the back of my heels. I sit in the plastic chair and wait for Finch.

Chapter Five

Tuesday, Day 1

A husky man wearing red nurse scrubs steps out from the nurses' area, holding my duffle bag. He turns to me and looks over the frame of his glasses that are perched on top of his nose. "You must be Sidra, right?" He says, double-checking the tag on the duffle bag. I nod. "Let's go, this won't take long." He shows a quick smile.

Pushing my feet further into my shoes, I stand up and jam all of my toes to the top. My feet drag along the floor as I try to keep my sneakers on. The man pushes open two large double doors. "This is the cafeteria. You enjoy your delicious three meals a day here with the other patients. Sometimes, small meetings are held here on special occasions. Do not come into the cafeteria without permission," He says, walking over to the table swinging his arms, causing my bag to fling back and forth. He places my bag on the table.

Taking a seat, I scoot in my chair as he digs into his shirt pocket. "I'm Finch; I help Katrina with the check-ins and watch over the patients throughout the day," he says, unfolding a sheet of paper. He smoothes out the paper on the edge of the table and pulls out a black pen from his pocket.

"Are you ready?"

"Yes."

He unzips my bag and lays out all of my pants on the table, counting each pair. "Seven lovely pants," he says, smiling. He pulls out three pairs of sweatpants from the pile and examines the waistbands. "Aw, I'm sorry you can't have drawstrings in your pants here, sweetheart," he says, twirling the drawstring around his thick index finger. Right, I forgot that anything string-like can be abused here. He pulls the drawstrings out from the small openings and places them to the side. "Would you like me to save these for you?" He asks, stroking his dark beard. It's going to be impossible to get the strings back in. There's no point in keeping them. My pants better stay up; I can't be showing off my bits. Who knows what kind of weirdos are staying here?

"You can throw them away."

"Okay then," he says as he reaches back into the bag, pulling out my shirts. "Ten shirts," he says, scribbling down the items and numbers. "Now, I can count out your panties, or you can count them without me laying a finger on them. I know how some ladies get about strange men touching their undies. The choice is all yours."

"Um, I don't mind if you touch them."

"Okay, here we go," he says, pulling out all my panties and bras. "Eight undies and bras."

Finch dumps the rest of the clothes from the bag onto the table. He pulls apart all my nightgowns. "Five nightgowns. These are good quality; they look comfortable to sleep in," He says, rubbing the material between his fingers.

Finch searches through my duffle bag again. He pulls out my fuzzy black house slippers. "Some patients would kill to have these," He says, logging them on the sheet of paper. My eyes widen. "Don't worry, it was just a joke," he says, laughing. The nurses here seem to enjoy teasing new patients a little too much.

"Oops, I almost forgot one pair of glasses, a hair tie, and a hair clip." He jots down the last of the items. "See, that took no time at all. I'll need your hair tie and clip, though," he says, extending his open hand to me. Pulling my tie out of the ponytail, my hair falls to my shoulders. I place it in the palm of his large hand.

"The flower clip, too."

"Please, you can't take this flower clip. It means so much to me," I say, pushing the lump in my throat down. My mom gave me this when we first met. I've worn it every day for 11 years. It reminds me that even though I was the worst kid there, she still wanted me and saw something in me that no one else did.

"Relax, sweetheart, let me look at it." Removing the flower clip from my hair, I place it in his palm. He pushes his glasses up to his eyes and examines it. Running his hands along the opening, he presses the end of it into his finger with force. "Good news, you can keep your clip," he says with a huge grin.

"Really? You won't get in trouble for letting me keep it?" I whisper

"Nope, it must be old because it's dull. But listen, keep it in your hair at all times, and do not lend it to anyone, or I will confiscate it from you until you are discharged. Do you understand?"

"Yes, thank you so much," I say, taking my clip back from him.

Sliding it back on the left side of my head, I press down, snapping it into place. "Let's hurry and get your stuff to your room so you can meet your peers. Katrina will take your bag back to the nurse's area. Let's go."

"Um, Finch, can I have a bag so I can take all my clothes?" I ask. He stands up, folding the piece of paper back up.

"That's a no, no. Patients aren't allowed to have any bag in their possession. They can quickly suffocate themselves," he says with an earnest look in his eyes.

He folds all my pants, shirts, and gowns. "Don't worry, sweetheart. I'll help you with your things. I've got these; you can carry your underwear and house slippers," he says, holding my clothes. Bunching up my underwear, I place my house shoes on top of the pile in my arms. Finch is so lovely; he reminds me of an older, wiser version of Bevan. Man, I miss them both already.

It makes me wonder, was Axel talking about Finch not liking him? I don't know them that well, but it's hard to believe he'd treat everyone so nicely and be mean to Axel.

He pushes one of the doors open with his foot, leaning his back against it. He holds it open, letting me exit first. "Another quick rule about food. No food or drinks whatsoever in the rooms. They will be thrown away if found. Snacks are to be eaten in the meeting room only," he says, walking ahead. I nod, trying not to trip on my sneakers.

"So, do we not take showers here? How does the whole hygiene thing work?" I ask.

"I was wondering when you'd ask. Don't worry. We provide you with a hygiene box with your name on it. It comes with a toothbrush, toothpaste, a hairbrush, a bar of soap, and shampoo. When you're ready for a shower, all you have to do is ask for your towels at the nurse's window. You must return your hygiene box after you take a shower." Talk about strict; it reminds me of my days in the group home.

"This is your room, number 7, remember that. We don't allow patients to visit other rooms, especially if you are of the opposite sex. The women are to the right side of the hall, and the men on the left." Finch pushes open the door, revealing a large room with four wooden-framed beds. A giant sealed window with metal mesh inside sits at the end of the room, flooding it with natural light.

"The first bed is yours," he says, placing my clothes on the plain old mattress. "When you're done putting away your clothes, you can come to the nurse's window and get your sheets, blankets, and pillowcase. Enjoy your stay at Pleasant Horizons!" He shouts, throwing his arms in the air, his face and voice cracking with fake excitement. Finch exits my new room.

Placing my panties and bras on the bed, I sit down on the rock-hard mattress. Next to the bed, two medium-sized brown cabinets with four shelves separate my bed from the bed across from mine. The bed across from mine is already made. It's been years since I've had a roommate. The last time I had one, she threw my boombox out the window and blamed me for it. Whoever shares this room with me better not touch my stuff, or we'll have an issue.

Flinging my clothes onto the first shelf of the cabinet, I shove my bras and panties onto the second shelf. Time to get the stuff to make up this rock slab they are passing off as a bed. Making my way down the hall, I peek into a few of the boys' rooms. A tall girl leaning against the wall stares at me as I step up to the nurse's window. Tapping on the window, I lean forward on my tiptoes, looking down onto the desk.

Great, the nurse behind the desk is sleeping. I'm starting to see why that Axel guy was upset earlier. Come on, wake up; I tap harder on the glass. The nurse lets out a small snort as she gets more comfortable. Are you serious? There's no way I'm sleeping on that bare mattress. Who knows what's been on that thing?

"You won't get her attention with those tiny taps," the girl leaning against the wall says.

"I don't think they'll like me banging on the window. The girl walks over to the window and makes a fist. She bangs on the window.

Chapter Six

Tuesday, Day 1

The red-haired nurse lifts her head, glaring at us both. She slides open the window.

"What do you ladies want? Can't you see I'm busy doing paperwork?"

"The new girl needs something, Zanna."

"What do you want?" Zanna asks, wiping some drool from the corner of her mouth.

"I just wanted my bedding. I didn't mean to bother you." Zanna gets out of her chair and makes her way to a big metal cabinet.

Turning to the girl standing next to me, I smile.

"Thanks for helping me. Um, I'm Sidra."

"I'm Nami, and don't worry about it. I had the same problem on my first day," she says, smiling.

"Here are your sheets, a blanket, and a pillowcase," Zanna says, handing them to me through the window. A strong, flowery perfume rises from the white sheets and the coarse blue blanket. At least it beats inhaling the smell of bleached blankets from the regular hospital. Zanna slides the window closed and lays her head back down on the desk. Her red hair drapes over her exhausted eyes.

"What room did you get assigned to?"

"Room 7," I say, walking away from her.

"That's my room. I finally have a roommate!" Nami shouts, catching up to me. Why's she so excited about that? I would love to have a whole room to myself. Just me, myself, and I. She walks beside me as her hot pink skirt sways back and forth. Her lengthy legs take long strides, making it hard for me to keep up.

"Why aren't you wearing socks or shoes? The floor looks cold," I say, looking down at her bare feet.

"Well, yeah, of course, the floor is cold. But I'd rather have cold toes than trip on my loose sneakers. If I fell in front of the others, I'd never live it down. Anyways, most of the others walk around with bare feet, too." That makes sense. Happy doesn't explain how grateful I am that Mom put my house shoes in my bag.

"Can I help you make up your bed? No one helped me, so I know how it feels getting those tissue-thin sheets on this nasty mattress," she says with rosy cheeks.

"Sure, I guess." She's so sweet that it's starting to become suspicious. She must be hiding something big. Putting my bedding down on the top of the cabinet, I grab the fitted sheet from the pile.

"I'll take this end," she says, grabbing the other end of the fitted sheet. We guide the sheet over to my bed and lay it down, pulling the edges over the corners of the mattress. Her long black hair, filled with loose curls, dangles over her shoulders as she maneuvers the sheet. "I'll grab the top sheet." Her white long-sleeved shirt becomes taut across her body. She stops reaching for the sheet and covers up her arms with her sleeves.

"Shoot, guess I couldn't reach it," she says, avoiding eye contact.

"Um, it's okay. I'll get it," I say, staring at her lanky arms. I wonder what she's hiding. Grabbing the top sheet, I unfold it and fling it in the air. The sheet flows down onto the bed like a feather. She smoothes out the wrinkles with her hand as the other holds down the ends of her sleeve.

"I can put the blanket on for you."

"The day is almost over. What's the point of making it neat when I'm going to mess it up in a few hours," I say, balling up the blanket and tossing it on the bed.

"Well, at least let me put your pillowcase on your pillow," she says, taking the bare pillow out from the bottom shelf of the cabinet.

"Okay, go for it," I say, kicking off my heavy sneakers. She slides the pillowcase over the lumpy old pillow. Sitting on my bed, I cross my legs.

"What happened in the real world to land you in here?"

"It's sort of a long story." Nami frowns, creating small wrinkles on her porcelain doll-like skin

"How about this: I'll tell you my boring story if you share your exciting tale," I offer

"I'm sure yours isn't boring. If you ended up here, something must have pushed you over the edge. To be honest, I hate sharing my personal stuff with the others here, so I get it."

"Yeah."

"Have you ever met someone and felt an instant bond or something like that?" She asks.

"Not really; I have too many trust issues. I must protect myself, you know?"

"Oh, well, I kind of felt it with you. Maybe I'm crazy, ha. Anyways, I'll share my story later."

My stomach interrupts with grumbles and groans.

"You've got to be super hungry. Don't say you aren't. I heard your stomach crying for help. I remember my first day, I was starving," she says, giggling.

"Yeah, I only had a couple of apple juices at the hospital. I'm guessing I've missed dinner, so I'll have to survive until breakfast time."

"Yep, too bad, they said they wouldn't be serving breakfast tomorrow because of the other's bad behavior," she says, covering her face.

"Damn, really?"

"Just kidding!" She shouts, trying to hide her laughter.

"Snack time is in 15 minutes, I think. Want to go to the meeting room and wait for it there?" she asks, pushing herself out of bed.

"You got me, and I almost believed the others were troublemakers."

"A few definitely are, but don't worry about it too much."

She straightens out her skirt as I put on my fuzzy house slippers. We walk down the hall towards the meeting room. "So, why are you happy that I'm your new roommate? Don't you like your own space?" I ask.

"It gets scary being in that big empty room. It's pitch black in there because the night staff closes all the doors to the rooms. It makes me paranoid. Now that you're here, it should take the edge off."

"I'm pretty lucky to have you as my roommate. In my mind, I imagined someone crazy sleeping across from me," I say, glancing over at her. Nami giggles as her cheeks become red.

She stops in front of the meeting room, "Ladies first," she says, extending her hand to the doorway. Nami's nice, but what about the others? As soon as I step into that room, they'll probably start staring at me. Dodging personal questions isn't a strength of mine. I'm sure their mouths are full, ready with questions.

"I can't do this," I mumble.

"Are you okay?" "I get anxious when I'm around too many people. I always feel different, out of the loop, you know? I'm barely capable of sharing what my name is," I say, backing away from the entrance of the meeting room.

She grabs my hand, "Sorry if touching makes you uncomfortable, but I want to show you I'm here. Yeah, I get it. We just met, but if I can help, I'm going to." She walks into the meeting room, still holding my hand. Following behind, my chest tightens.

"We can sit here," she says, sitting down on the torn burgundy sofa. Sitting down, my butt sinks into a massive hole in the distressed couch. Pieces of cotton burst through several cracks of fake leather. To my left, a small burgundy sofa sits in the corner, facing a counter with a tray full of juice boxes. Damn, this place is torn up. It's clear the people who stay here don't respect themselves or the hospital property. That's probably why the TV's in a cage.

"Feeling better?" She whispers into my ear.

"My body is so clenched I could rip this couch with my butt. If you weren't here, I'd still be in the room."

"Let's play a game to get your mind off the stress." I nod.

"I'm going to guess how old you are. I'm thinking you're 25."

My eyes widen, "I look that old? I'm 18." I say, laughing.

"Oh, I just wanted to make you laugh," she says, grinning.

"Okay, my turn to guess. Hm, are you 16?"

"Nope, I'm 18. People must be telling the truth when they say I have a baby face. If I were 16, I'd be on the teen side. That's what Katrina told me when she guessed that I was 15. We're barely legal," Nami says, giggling.

"Teen side? That's kind of sad to think about pre-teens and teens trying to kill themselves. Did Katrina tell you what it's like over there?"

"No, but I do hear them talking about how crazy the teenagers can get." If they have a teen side and an adult side, they definitely have a kid side. It must be hell on earth for some kids if they want to kill themselves. The only thing I can do from here is to pray for their beautiful little souls to be saved.

"Come get your snacks, guys!" Katrina shouts from the hall.

"Finally! I'll go and get the snacks. You wait here, okay," Nami says, walking out of the room. What's the snack going to be? Please be chips, no trail mix, mm, or pizza rolls. My mouth begins to water. Axel makes his way into the meeting room and takes a seat on the smaller couch. Staring at the side of his face, I try to take another look at his gorgeous eyes.

"If you stare any harder, you'll burn a hole in his face," Nami says, towering over me.

"I told you I'm not good around people. Making a good time awkward is almost like my superpower." Nami sits down laughing.

"It's okay. Here's your snack. Try not to eat it too fast," she says, handing me a cookie wrapped in a thin brown napkin.

"Thanks."

"No problem," she says, smiling with a mouth full of cookie.

Removing the napkin from around the cookie, the loose crumbs rain onto my lap. Turning the cookie around, I examine all the chocolate chips.

"Eat the damn cookie already!" Axel shouts from the couch. Looking up from my cookie, his pearl-gray eyes lock onto mine.

"She can stare at her cookie all she wants. Why were you even watching her in the first place? That's creepy, man," Nami blurts out. He turns his head away from us, not saying a word.

"Thanks, I would have said something stupid if you didn't jump in."

"Don't even thank me. Guys are jerks sometimes."

Shoving the whole cookie in my mouth, I let the chocolate chips coat my tongue. This is the best cookie ever. The food here must be good. I can't wait to try breakfast.

"Want to head back to our room so we can get ready for bed?"

"Yeah, sure," I say, getting up, shaking the crumbs off my shirt. She takes my trash from my hand and tosses it in the bin. We make our way down the hall to our room. Lying on my bed, I curl up under my blanket. It's setting in now. Being with strangers and sleeping on this rock, if I knew this would have happened, I wouldn't have looked at those pills. She crawls into her bed and closes her eyes. A night shift nurse flicks the light off and closes the door.

"Are you okay?" I ask.

"Yeah, it's not as scary."

"Good, sleep well."

Chapter Seven

Wednesday, Day 2

"Wake up, ladies!" Finch hollers from the doorway. Rubbing my eyes, they adjust to the bright fluorescent lights. The sun isn't even out yet. What time is it? Turning over to avoid the light, Nami cuddles her pillow.

"Nami, wake up," I say, wiping my glasses with the edge of my shirt. Placing them back on my face, I stretch out my back. If Mom saw me wake up with my glasses on, she'd be upset big time. Something about breaking or bending them during sleep, but whatever: she's not here.

"Nami!" I shout.

"What!?"

"We have to get ready. It's my first day, and I don't want to start out missing meetings. Besides, you're the only kind of cool thing here. So, um, it would be, um, nice to have you around," I say, getting out of bed.

"Ugh, if I could change one thing about this place, it'd be not waking up at 6 am," she whines into her pillow. "Looks like you slept like a brick on that rock."

"It felt amazing. All thanks to you," she says, flashing a toothy smile.

"Can I take a shower before you? I feel gross. I haven't had one in a couple of days," I say, feeling sticky with sweat.

"Go ahead, but can you grab my hygiene box, too, while you're up there?"

"Sure," I say, sliding on my slippers. My feet drag along the smooth floor as I make my way over to the nurse's window. Zanna walks into the nurse's station with her purse and lunchbox. Knocking on the window three times, I catch her attention. Zanna slams open the window.

"You already want something? Aren't you new? You shouldn't be asking for stuff yet. I can't even have five minutes to myself," she says, putting her bags on the desk.

"I'm sorry, but I just want my hygiene box and towels so I can take a shower."

"What's your name?" she asks, digging into her ear with her pinkie finger.

"Sidra, also, can you give me Nami's too?"

"Wait, give me a second." Turning around, I look through the meeting room window. Fears, secrets, and regrets have been spilled in that room. Today, that room will be dry because I'm not going to spill anything out to these people.

"Take your boxes and go. Try not to bother me; I've got a lot of work today."

"Thank you," I say, taking the boxes and towels from her.

"Hey, I got our boxes and-"

"Surprise! I made up your bed," Nami says, straightening the blanket.

"You didn't have to do that."

"Yeah, I know, but you got the boxes."

"Thank you. I don't deserve your kindness."

"Here's your box and towels. I'll jump in the shower; thank you again," I say, grabbing my outfit for the day. Walking into the bathroom, I place my clothes on the small sink.

"Why doesn't the bathroom have a door?" I ask.

"I don't know, I found it weird, too. I always feel like one of the boys will sneak into the room and take a peek at me in the shower."

"Another reason to have a roommate, huh?" I ask laughing

"Definitely." Of course, there are no shower curtains. No wonder they give you all these towels so you don't bust your butt on the wet floor. Turning the handle to the left and then right, I pull and then push.

"How do you turn this stupid thing on!?"

"Let me help you," Nami giggles as she comes into the bathroom. She pulls on the handle and then jerks it to the left. Water shoots out from the showerhead, moistening the tiles below.

"There you go, enjoy."

"Thanks," I say, placing my glasses on the sink. Removing my clothes, I grab the thin bar of soap with the washrag. The water pelts my tender skin. They worry about doors, socks, laces, and curtains hurting us, but they don't think twice about water pressure. At this rate, this water will blast all the dirt off of me without me having to use any soap. Washing every inch of my body with the mild soap, I rinse off all the suds. My hands search for the small towel as I step out of the shower. A mirror made of reflective plastic stares at me as I put my glasses on. My distorted reflection mixes with the graffiti engraved into the mirror. I'm glad I can barely see myself. Finishing up my daily hygiene, I readjust the flower clip in my hair.

"Where do I put my dirty towels?" I ask.

"You can put them next to the door. The cleaning staff will get them later." Dropping my damp towels on the floor, I push them next to the door with my foot.

"Can you wait for me to finish? I want to return our boxes together, then head straight to the cafeteria."

"Sure, it's best you go with me anyway. Zanna scares me,

"I say, chucking my dirty clothes ball onto the last shelf of my cabinet. Sitting on my bed, I gaze out the large window. The sun continues to rise, making the sky turn a dusty orange. Once I get out of this place, my family will be like an annoying paparazzi gang shoving all their questions in my face, expecting me to answer or even fall apart. No one's ever tried to kill themselves in my family. We don't even talk about mental health. As long as they don't blame this on Mom, I think I'll be okay. It wasn't her fault; she was clueless like the rest of them. "Almost done. I just have to brush my hair," Nami announces from the bathroom.

"What's the first meeting like?" She walks out of the bathroom, brushing her long, wet, curly hair.

"It's almost like a pre-meeting. It's pretty boring, though. It gets everyone in the mindset to talk about their feelings or whatever. If there are new people, we introduce ourselves to one another. Nothing too serious to start with."

"Yeah, doesn't sound too bad," I say, getting out of bed.

"Alright, I'm ready," she says, throwing her soiled towels on top of mine. Nami carries both boxes as we walk down the hall. The scent of sweet pancakes surrounds us. She walks up to the window and knocks on the glass hard. Zanna opens the window, glaring at us as Nami hands her the boxes.

"Bye," Zanna says, slamming the window. I don't know what we were expecting her to say. A thank you for returning your box would have been nice, or have a lovely breakfast. What's with the female nurses here? Walking through the cafeteria doors, the aroma of pancakes grows stronger.

"The food is good here, right?" Nami snickers.

"What's that supposed to mean?" I ask.

"Hey, good morning," Finch says, holding a chipped clipboard. A tall metal rack holding several red trays sits next to him.

"Step right up to get your flavorful meal," he says, gesturing at Nami. Finch hands her a red tray then scribbles down on his clipboard. Stepping forward, he hands me my tray.

"Thanks." Finch smiles. Nami leads me to a table in the far back of the cafeteria. A plastic plate covers the top of the food. A plastic fork and napkin sit between the plate and a small carton of orange juice. Surprisingly, they let us use forks. I'm sure this could do some damage to someone's eyes if used right. Removing the top plate, I set it aside. Scrambled eggs, a slice of bacon, a small sausage link, and two small oval-shaped pancakes are grouped in the middle of the plate. Grabbing my fork, I pierce through the sausage link. Sinking my teeth into the sausage, salty, burnt pieces spread out over my tongue. Sticking my tongue out, I try wiggling the taste off.

"Does the sausage taste weird to you?"

"I haven't tried it yet. It looks off," Nami says. Pushing the sausage off my fork, I turn my attention to the bright yellow eggs. Using my fingers, I scoop a few chunks of scrambled eggs onto my fork. The eggs enter my mouth, bursting into liquid powder between my teeth.

"You look constipated. Is the food not good?" she asks with a crooked smile.

"The eggs are interesting. I'm sure the pancakes will be amazing, though." My stomach gurgles and aches

"You know what, never mind. This food is trash," I say, pushing my tray away.

"Haha, that's why I only took a few bites of the pancake. The food here is so unbelievably nasty. Me and the others live off of snacks between meals. If we didn't, we'd be stuck in the bathroom all day."

"Thanks for telling me after I put it in my mouth," I say, smiling. She lowers her head,

"I'm sorry. I wanted to see if you'd like it without my opinion. I wasn't trying to be mean."

"You weren't being mean. I'm sorry if that came out the wrong way. Really, it's okay, don't be sad," I say, trying to defuse the situation. She raises her head, showing a faint smile.

"You can have my orange juice," I say, sliding it to her. Her smile becomes brighter as she opens the orange juice. "Orange is the best juice." "My juice of choice is apple," I say, licking my lips.

"Maybe one day we should mix them and see what it tastes like."

"Okay, but you're trying it first," I say, laughing.

"Thanks for making me smile."

"Doesn't this food remind you of school lunches? I don't know about you, but my school lunches were always awful.

"Yeah...school...," she mumbles as she pats one of her arms

"Are you okay?"

"Yeah, I hate school. It's sort of why I'm here," she says, avoiding eye contact. "The first meeting of the day starts in 10 minutes, ladies and gentlemen. Finish your breakfast quickly, but don't choke!" Finch yells out. Katrina slaps Finch on the arm. He looks at her with a goofy face.

"Hey, let's go before the sofa seats get taken," Nami says, tossing out her trash. Tossing my food in the garbage, I place my tray back on the metal rack. We walk into the meeting room together and sit on the big sofa. Axel flops down on the smaller couch and lies on his back, leaving no seats for the others. The other patients make their way into the room, pulling out the plastic chairs around the table. They place them next to the sofas, creating an oddly shaped circle.

"Who runs the first meeting?" I ask Nami.

"Katrina. She's nice once you get to know her," she says, tucking her right foot under her left thigh.

My stomach tightens as anxiety makes itself at home in my head. You can do this. They won't be asking serious questions like Nami said. They want to know my name and what kind of things I like. You've been through a lot worse. It's just small talk.

Chapter Eight

Wednesday, Day 2

"Good morning, everyone," Katrina says, pushing an office chair between two other patients.

"Looks like we have a new person here," she says, smiling. My heart skips a beat. "Since we have someone new today, I will reintroduce myself. My name is Katrina. I run the first meeting every morning and take care of you all, whether you like it or not."

Katrina looks at me. "What's your name?"

"Sidra."

"And how old are you?" she asks as if she didn't already know the answer.

"I'm, um, 18."

"Okay, everyone, say hi to Sidra. You were all new once, so don't be jerks," Katrina says, looking at everyone. The room falls silent. Expecting someone to say hi, I look at them all. Even Nami is quiet. Why are they avoiding me? Do I look weird? "Come on, guys! That's just rude. Since you all have lost your voice, I'll make it easy for you. Everyone in this room will say their name and how old they are," Katrina commands—a collective sigh floods from everyone's mouths. "Oh, so that's how you feel. Well, now you have to state why you're here, too," she adds.

Katrina points to a broad-chested man sitting to her left, "Hurry up, spit it out."

The man's bronze skin gleams under the lights. Rubbing his bald head, the man clears his throat. A sigh passes through his lips, "Hi, my name is Talon. I'm 30. I'm here because I lost my job," he says in a deep, rusty voice. It must have been an amazing job.

"Next, let's keep this moving," Katrina says, clapping her hands at us.

"Hi, I'm Felice, I'm 24. I'm stuck here today because I lost someone very special to me," she says in a hushed tone. Her hoodie covers the majority of her face, only revealing her emerald eyes.

"Hey! I'm Nami, I'm 18. I'm here because some stuff happened at school and with my mom, making me want to die." That's so vague. Her story was the only one that interested me. Maybe I can play it cool like that. Seems like everyone is pissed about sharing, so maybe they'll be grateful if I keep it short.

"You guys need to work on expanding on what happened. This isn't a guessing game," Katrina says, annoyed.

"I'll try better next time," Nami says

"Anyways, Sidra, it's your turn. You're the star of the hour," Katrina says, leaning forward in her chair. Everyone's eyes shift to me.

"Can I, um, go last?"

"Yeah, let her go last; she's just going to waste our time as she soul-searches for the obvious answer," Axel says.

"Check yourself, Axel," Katrina snaps

Axel rolls his eyes, making himself more comfortable on the couch.

"You know what? I'll go. I'm 18, I'm here because people who I thought loved me abandoned me."

"And what else? I'm not taking any more short answers," Katrina demands.

"So, I tried to jump off the roof, and all of you already know my name, even the new girl," Axel says. That sounds all too familiar, well, not the part about jumping from the roof.

"Okay, well, you're next," Katrina says, looking at a young man to her right.

"Sup girl, I'm Daric, I'm 22. I got hella drunk and tried to jump into traffic because my brain won't leave me alone...," he says, pushing his butterscotch blond hair from his tired eyes. His pale skin reveals a long, dark scar that runs from the base of his neck to his chest. "What do you mean your brain won't leave you alone?" Katrina asks.

"My therapist said I have something called PTSE or somethin."

"PTSD," Nami blurts out

"Yeah, that," Daric nods

"Why are y'all looking at me like that? You don't know a lick about me, see I hate this sharing crap," Daric blurts out.

"Relax, I think everyone is just wondering what may have caused you to get PTSD. This is supposed to help, not turn into a fight club. I must say I'm disappointed in all of you. You were all welcomed in by others when you were new. They shared some very intimate things with you to help you feel less alone. I expected you to do the same for Sidra without the pushback," Katrina says, shaking her head.

"But I-"

"Stop talking, Axel!" Katrina hollers

His eyes begin to water, he turns over on his side hiding his face.

Katrina takes a deep breath, then looks at me, "Sidra, please share with us why you're here."

"I guess it all piled up, me being abused, then abandoned, having to survive the foster care system. Then, them wanting me to be back in their lives, I couldn't take it, so I overdosed on my medication," I say, not letting any more information slip out.

"Who are they?" Katrina asks, leaning forward in her chair.

"My biological parents."

Axel turns over and looks at me with wide eyes. His stare intensifies.

"Thanks, everyone, for sharing. Remember, we can't help if you keep hiding your wounds. That's it for the first meeting. Talk amongst yourselves until the next meeting starts," Katrina says, pushing the office chair out of the room. Axel gets up from the couch, following Katrina.

"That was rough," Nami says, placing her hand on my shoulder.

"Yeah, not at all how I'd imagined it would go."

"Do you have any idea why Axel was staring at you like that?"

"No, but is he always this disrespectful?"

"Not like today. Usually, Katrina has it under check, but I guess it escalated a bit too quickly. Word around here is that Katrina has a soft spot for him, so she puts up with him the most."

Forget Axel, he's just a brat. Daric makes me feel uneasy. The way he snapped at me for looking at him. What is he capable of?

"You look a little freaked out, but I have some news that might make you happy."

"What is it?"

"The next meeting is super fun. The lady who runs it is kind of weird but nice. She lets us do arts and crafts while we listen to music. Sometimes she brings in games," she says with a huge smile.

"That does sound fun; anything to take my mind off the first meeting, I'm fine with."

"Watch my seat for a second; I have to pee so bad," Nami says, jumping off the couch.

Just breathe; you may be in here by yourself, but it doesn't seem too bad. My breathing becomes heavier.

"Boo!" Axel shouts in my ear.

Jumping, I clench, trying to hide my fear.

"We need to talk," he says, sitting in Nami's seat.

"Um, hi."

"Open your hand," he says with a creepy smile.

He shoves a folded piece of paper in my half-open hand.

"Read it," he whispers. Nami walks into the room, towering over Axel.

"Move," she says in a low tone.

Axel gets up from the couch and walks into the hallway.

"Was he harassing you, man? I knew he was creepy," she says, sitting back in her spot.

"Not exactly. He shoved this paper in my hand."

"Oh my gosh! That looks like a love letter," she says, letting out a slight squeal.

"Okay, wait. He barely knows me. It can't be."

"You'll never know if you don't open it."

Unfolding the paper, the message written in blue ink reads: *Foster kid, uh? It's always nice meeting people who know about the awful things that happen to kids in the system. Meet me at dinner. Find me and sit down. Try not to draw too much attention to yourself.*

Nami stares at me with excitement in her eyes.

"Nope, there is no way I'm meeting him at dinner. He can forget it, " I say, balling up the note.

"Aw, but why not? It sounds genuine."

"So what? Why would I want to talk about my foster care experience to a spoiled brat? For all we know, he probably doesn't even know about the system," I say.

"I'm sorry. I didn't mean to work you up like that."

"It's not you. I just got here; I'm not sure how hard people try to hear about others' secrets. I'm in protective mode. Look, I'll think about it. It would be nice to talk to someone else who has probably experienced what I did. No judgment, just empathy," I say, putting the note in my pocket.

Chapter Nine

Wednesday Day, 2

A narrow-figured woman walks through the doorway, pushing a large gray cart filled with various art supplies and board games. A round black radio sits on the very top of a tall stack of papers. Her strong perfume fills the room, assaulting my nostrils.

"Everyone ready to have some fun!" She shouts.

"Is she normally this excited about the group?" I whisper.

"Yep, it's like she drinks too many cups of coffee before she comes into work," Nami says, trying to hide her laugh.

"A new person! Hi, my name is Bel. I provide fun activities to help you get to know yourself and others better," she says, tucking her gray button-down shirt into her black jeans.

"Hi, um, I'm Sidra."

"Nice to meet you," she says, smiling.

"For today's art lesson, we're going to be making portraits of each other! Doesn't that sound fun?" Bel asks.

"Not really, sounds annoying," Daric says, touching his scar.

"Don't be such a baby. I'm sure the new girl thinks you're cute," Axel says with a wicked smile. Daric looks at me. Avoiding his gaze, I look down at my hands.

"I'll break you off into pairs. Let's see, Nami and Sidra. Daric and Felice. Axel and Talon. Get close to your partners. When you're ready, you can come get paint, chalk, or markers to create your masterpiece," Bel says.

"What's this supposed to do for us?" Talon asks, grabbing a sheet of construction paper with a box of markers.

"It helps with seeing yourself through others' eyes. Reflect with your partner about features you like or that you never noticed about your face or theirs. Changing your perspective about yourself can help release some hidden insecurities. Remember, be polite." Damn, if I got Axel, I would have tried to draw his amazing eyes. On second thought, it wouldn't be worth it if he just ended up calling me ugly or something.

"I'll get our paper. Do you want markers or paint?" she asks, standing.

"I'll take paint."

"Okay. This is going to be so fun," she says, hurrying to the cart. Talon leans towards Axel, squinting hard at his facial features. With light, feathery strokes, Talon sketches out Axel's hair. Nami settles on the couch again. She hands me a sheet of pink construction paper, setting aside a green one for herself. She places a small paint kit, complete with a thin plastic paintbrush, in my hand.

"Is green your favorite color too?" I ask, facing her.

"Nope. I grabbed it to match your hair clip. Pink is my favorite."

"Purple used to be my favorite, but it shifted to green. There's something about green. It's so bright, I guess my eyes crave it because I feel like I'm being surrounded by dar- Um, never mind. Thanks for grabbing the stuff."

"It's okay..."

"We should get started, " I say, fixing my eyes on my paper. "Yep." Bel places a CD in the radio and turns it on. Soft classical music plays as everyone focuses on their portraits. Felice's nose and mouth peek out from her hood, still covering most of her face. Daric draws thick lines for her face and eyes. He shades them in with green chalk. Her head pops up for a few seconds each time as she sketches me with a steady hand. Looking back down at my blank paper, I begin to paint her long, black, curly hair. Her big, round eyes and button nose rest inside a horribly painted round face. The only thing that looks right in this painting is her hair. Art is not for me, but it's nice. It reminds me of all the activities we used to do in the group home. Every weekend, when my mom came to visit me, I'd give her whatever I had made that week. She loved everything I made. Stealing a quick glimpse at Nami's portrait, I watch her trace over her light pencil lines with black paint.

"Five more minutes, everyone. Be ready to share the things you've learned about yourself and your partner," Bel says, walking around looking at everyone's art. This meeting, compared to earlier, is like paradise. For some reason, I thought maybe Axel would ruin this one, too. He looks like he is enjoying himself, though. There's no way my entire stay will be like this, but I can dream.

"I'm almost done. I can't wait to show you," Nami says with a huge smile.

"I wish I could say the same. I think you're so pretty, but my hands don't know how to express it on paper. Please don't get offended when you see mine."

"You think I'm pretty?" Tears crowd themselves in Nami's eyes.

"Times up. Who would like to go first?" Bel asks, leaning against the cart. Talon's hand shoots into the air.

"Let's see what you and Axel did." Talon and Axel show their portraits to everyone.

"Axel has incredible features. He looks sophisticated. If he didn't have a Mohawk, he'd be hired in a heartbeat," Talon says, pointing at the picture.

"Maybe that's why I got the Mohawk. Looking like a boring businessman doesn't work for me," Axel says. His happy expression melts into a displeased look.

"We all know Talon by his bald head, but have any of you noticed that when he smiles, he has a small dimple on the left side of his mouth?" Axel says, pointing to it in his picture.

"Really?" Talon asks, touching around his mouth.

"Smile," Nami says. Talon smiles. A slight indentation appears next to his mouth.

"Well, look at that! Well done, Axel. Talon, how does it make you feel that you never noticed that feature before?" Bel asks.

"Stupid. When I worked as a market research analyst, I made sure I looked good every morning. You have to look your best when meeting high-paying clients. I'd have crisp, clean suits, and I was always clean-shaven and smelling good. All that time in the mirror, and I never noticed it," he says, rubbing the stubble on his face.

"Did you ever take the time to smile at yourself in the mirror?" Bel asks.

"No, it's hard to smile when everything but your job is falling apart around you."

"Would you like to explain a bit more?" Talon stares at us as we all wait for him to speak.

"No. I'm done sharing," Talon says, slumping down in his chair.

"Good job, you two. Daric and Felice, you're up." Bel says. They both show their portraits.

"Yo, Felice actually has a face. If you lived in my hood, my boys would be fallin' for those eyes," Daric says, holding up his picture.

"Aw, that's sweet, I think," Nami says. "Daric's scar makes him look badass," Felice says in a hushed tone.

"I look like a monster, but thanks for tryin'," Daric says.

"Why do you think you look like a monster?" Bel asks.

"Man, no one ever wants to talk to a guy like me. Ew, look at his nasty scar, or don't get near him. He looks dangerous, is all I hear. My boys are the only ones who accept me."

"Boys?" Talon asks.

"It ain't yo damn business," Daric snaps. Felice crumbles up her picture and throws it on the floor. She curls up in her chair, covering her face.

"Let's all breathe for a second," Bel says, grabbing the balled-up picture off the floor.

"Can we go now?" Nami asks, raising her hand.

"Yes," Bel says. She shows her portrait first. My painted, soft-brown face lies elegantly on the green paper. Shading and highlights bring my eyes and hair to life. It's gorgeous. Everyone's eyes light up with excitement as they stare at her picture.

"It's beautiful, Nami," Bel says in awe.

"Why didn't you draw her glasses?" Axel asks.

"Because Sidra looks so beautiful with or without them. I wanted her to know that," Nami says with a smile.

"I...I... don't know what to say, but thank you."

"Let's see yours, Sidra," Bel says. Showing my portrait to everyone, I look at their unimpressed faces.

"Nami's hair and rosy cheeks make her, um, look like a model. Her skin is clear and, um, perfect." Axel and Daric burst out laughing.

"Yo, why do you make Nami look like a potato with long hair? " Daric blurts out. "Nami drew you like a movie star, and you draw her like a mutated spud! I can't breathe, oh my gosh," Axel says, howling with laughter. Tears run down my face as my chest burns with regret.

"Shut up! She tried her best. You guys act like you made masterpieces when a ten-year-old could have done better, " Nami yells. She wipes the tears from my face with the sleeves of her shirt. "It's okay, Sidra; I like your picture. No one has ever said I looked like a model." Axel watches as more tears pour out of my eyes.

"I'm sorry, I didn't mean... I'm sorry," he says softly. Turning away from Axel, I wipe my face.

"Axel and Daric, that was very uncalled for. I asked everyone to be polite. I'm disappointed in you two," Bel says with anger in her eyes.

"What? It's just a picture. Why is she taking it so hard?" Daric asks. Bel snatches all the markers, chalk, and paint from everyone and packs them back on the cart. She turns off the radio.

"Today's meeting was going so well. I'm sorry, Sidra, please feel better; I'll see you tomorrow," Bel says, pushing her arts and crafts cart out of the room.

"Lunch is going to be starting soon. Maybe in about 30 minutes," Nami says, holding my hand.

"Okay."

"Maybe some food will make you feel better."

"Maybe." Nami glares at Axel.

"I'm keeping your picture, and I'm going to hang it in my room when I get home," Nami says, taking the painting from my hands.

"When are you leaving?"

"I see my psychiatrist tomorrow. He's going to let me know if I get to go home Saturday," she says, smiling.

"I'm happy for you..."

"I see the food rack coming!" Talon shouts, looking out of the meeting room window.

"Good, get me out of this depressing room," Felice says, stretching in her chair.

"Let's go eat; you'll feel better soon," Nami says, helping me off the couch. I nod.

Chapter Ten

Wednesday Day, 2

Everyone makes their way back to the meeting room. The smell of cheap pizza sauce and cheese lingers in the air. Small burps slip from Daric's lips as I take my seat on the large couch. She joins me, rubbing her stomach.

"How do you mess up pizza?" Nami asks.

"I kind of liked the rubbery cheese. It reminds me of the pizza they used to serve at school."

"Oh yeah, the ones cut into squares," Nami says, remembering

"What's the third group about?"

"You know, stuff like how to deal with your feelings. It's boring." Felice curls up on the small sofa next to Axel. A small smile peeks out from her hood. Smiling back, I look over at Axel. His head hangs low.

"Are you feeling better?" Nami asks.

"Yeah. I was thinking about dinner with Axel."

"I don't think you should go. He made you upset. He's lucky I didn't kick him in his balls," Nami says, clenching her jaw. Nami kicking him in his gems would have been a sight to see. Since the meeting, he hasn't spoken to anyone. Not even Katrina. Now I feel bad. I wasn't trying to be dramatic. Axel looks at me for a second and turns away.

"Sorry, everyone, am I late?" A muscular man asks from the doorway.

"Whoa," slips from my mouth. Nudging me with her elbow, Nami winks.

"Yep, but thank you for shaving off twenty minutes of group. It's already been a long day," Talon says. The man takes a chair from the table and sits down, completing the odd circle.

"Why do you say that?" The man asks, adjusting his glasses. Talon looks at me and back at the man.

"We got a new chick. She was crying earlier," Daric says.

"Oh well, hello, I'm Lawton. What's your name?"

"Si-Sidra."

"Nice to meet you. I'm sorry to hear that you were upset earlier. Maybe I can help with that. I teach about coping skills that you can utilize during everyday life," he says, showing off a white smile.

"Give her some of those coping skills or something. I hate seeing people cry," Talon says.

"What's wrong with crying?" Felice asks, sitting up. Her emerald eyes latch onto Talon.

"Nothing," Talon replies with a worried look. Felice curls back up, covering her face.

"There is absolutely nothing wrong with crying. I want everyone here to know that. It helps to purify aches and pains in the heart," Lawton says.

"Why does crying bother you so much, Talon?" Nami asks.

"I have my reasons. It's not going to help your mental health if I tell you about my business."

"Jeez, sorry," Nami says, rolling her eyes.

"Correction. Sharing your experiences can help someone else more than you know. Keep that in mind, Talon," Lawton corrects.

"Sorry." The room falls silent as Lawton takes out papers from his bag.

"I brought some worksheets for you all today," Lawton says, handing the sheets to Axel.

"Take one and pass it around," he adds. Axel takes a worksheet and passes the rest on to the others. Felice hands the papers to me. Taking one, I pass the rest to Nami. One large bubble sits in the middle of the paper, surrounded by three smaller bubbles.

"What I want you all to do now is fill in the large bubble. Put one thing that makes you sad, angry, and anxious," Lawton says, getting up from his chair. He hands out three-inch pencils without erasers to everyone. Tapping the pencil on my thigh, I pretend to think. Axel scribbles down a few words as Daric pokes multiple holes around the bubbles with his pencil. Maybe I should put down something. Getting called out for not participating in the group would make things worse. Liars make me angry, people constantly judging me makes me anxious, and being left behind makes me sad. Am I not good enough? Glancing over at Nami's paper, I try to make out the words covered by her hair. If my parents hadn't given me up, I would never have turned out like this. Foster brothers, sisters, and parents wouldn't have hurt me. I could have been someone amazing, but they ruined it all.

"Is everyone done?" Lawton asks, looking around the room.

"Yeah," Daric says, holding up his hole-filled paper. Everyone else nods.

"Sidra, since you are new, you can be the first to share," Lawton says, smiling. My heart drops to my feet. Bringing my paper close to my face, I cover the anxiety boasting in my eyes.

"Liars, people, and um being abandoned."

"What do you mean?" Felice asks quietly.

"Um, liars make me mad, people judging makes me uncomfortable, and people abandoning me hurts."

"Thank you for giving us more details," Lawton says. Everyone's eyes shift away from my face. My heart settles in my chest as a steady, calm washes over me.

"Felice, you're up," Lawton says.

"Thinking of my baby boy that I lost makes me sad. My ex-boyfriend makes me so mad. I guess people asking me about my family makes me anxious." "Thank you, Felice. Axel, you're next."

"Neglectful parents piss me off. Seeing little kids being mistreated hurts, and feeling helpless all the time makes me anxious."

"You haven't shared like this in a while, Axel. I'm proud of you," Lawton says. Axel looks down at his hands.

"Looks like you're up, Talon."

"When my wife nags me every minute, that makes me angry. When she threatens to take the kids, that makes me anxious. Lo-"

"Haha, it's because you beat her," Daric says, smirking.

"Excuse you?"

"Why else would she run with the kids?" Daric asks. Talon shoots up from his chair. His muscles twitch as he leans towards Daric's face.

"I never hit my wife! You know nothing about me or my family!" He hollers.

"Why are you so damn mad then? Hit me like you hit your kid, Dad!" Talon lunges forward, grabbing Daric by the shirt.

"Knock it off!" Lawton says, jumping between them.

"You should be in jail. Your wife hates you!" Daric yells over Lawton's shoulder.

"Me in jail!? You deserve that hideous scar on your neck, you freak!" Talon yells out. Daric places his hand on his scar as he stares blankly at the wall.

"Please stop!" Felice cries out, grabbing Talon's arm. She pulls him away from Daric and Lawton.

"What's going on here?!" Finch shouts, walking into the room. Everyone quiets down as heavy breathing takes the place of yelling.

"Daric was provoking Talon, and they almost got in a fight," Lawton says, putting down his arms.

"Daric, come to me," Finch says, gesturing to him. Daric walks up to Finch with tears in his eyes.

"You cannot join us for the next meeting. Apologize to Talon now and go to your room."

"S-sorry, Talon," Daric says, looking at the floor. Talon takes a seat. Tears fall into his hands as he tries to cover his face.

"I would never, I would never," Talon says, shaking. Axel leaves the room as everyone takes a seat. Nami looks at me with fear. She grabs my hand. "I'm sorry you all had to see that. Now you know why coping skills are important. We'll finish the worksheets tomorrow. I'll try to be on time," Lawton says, collecting the worksheets. Felice wipes away Talon's tears with her delicate hands. Lawton walks out of the room, rubbing the back of his neck. "I'm sorry, everyone. I should have stayed calm, but..."

"You don't need to apologize. He knew what he was doing when he started instigating," I say.

"I agree," Nami adds.

"Did you hear Daric call Talon Dad?" Nami whispers.

"Yeah, it was a little weird."

"Anyways, you'll love the next meeting. We get to go outside," Nami says, smiling.

"What? They let us roam around outside of the hospital?" She giggles,

"No, it's like a park, but it's still inside the hospital. You'll see." Finch pokes his head into the meeting room,

"Time for the next group."

"Follow me," Nami says, standing. Everyone follows Nami into the hall. They all line up as Finch drags a bag of sports balls behind him.

"Get ready for the greatest group of the day!" He shouts. His voice echoes down the hall.

"So, are your arms doing better, Nami?" Finch whispers.

"Yeah, thanks." Nami rubs her arm.

"Let's get this party started," Finch says, leading the line. Taking a few steps forward, Finch trips over the bag of sports balls. Snickering and muffled laughter fill the hall. He shakes the embarrassment off and swings the bag of balls over his shoulders. He leads us down the hall and makes a sharp left turn. "We have arrived," Finch says, unlocking a purple door. He pushes it open just a bit. Sunlight illuminates the hallway.

Chapter Eleven

Wednesday Day, 2

Walking along the pebble path, the green grass sways in the warm breeze. A small bench area sits underneath an old canopy.

"Since you're new, welcome to our little slice of outside! It's not that big, but it's the favorite group amongst most, if not all, the patients," Finch says, dropping the bag down on the grass. Wow, it's like the size of a one-bedroom apartment. Doing several cartwheels, Nami flops down on the grass, giggling. The fresh air rejuvenates my lungs as the sun's rays welcome my depleted skin. Axel, Finch, and Talon toss around a worn-out foam football. Shouts, laughter, and heavy breaths fill the small park.

"Felice want to hang out with us?" Nami asks. Shaking her head, Felice takes a seat on one of the benches. Felice's eyes fix themselves on the guys playing with the foam ball. Sitting down, the grass crunches underneath my weight. Nami sits in front of me, pulling up a few pieces of grass.

"This mini-park is great, huh?" she asks with a huge smile.

"It's awesome. It's a nice little breather."

"Remember yesterday when I said I'd tell you my story? Well, I think I'm ready."

"Are you sure? I don't want you to feel like you have to?"

"I know, but so much has happened today. Seeing Talon and Daric shout out personal things for everyone to hear bothered me. I started thinking if that happened to me, I wouldn't want you to hear about me through someone else's mouth," she says.

"Oh, I didn't know it affected you so much. Go ahead, tell me, it's a lovely day out. There's no better time than now."

"My mom hates me. She treats me like I'm not hers. She is a narcissistic monster. She loves to remind me that she is in control of every single thing in my life. My mother enjoys trampling on my dreams of becoming an artist because she would rather I stay home and be her servant. I can't even have friends, even if I wanted them, I couldn't have any because I would get bullied at school. She never cared when I told her that school was hard and that everyone hated me. My dad is the only one who cares, but he is also under her control. I don't know why he stays with her, but it's hurting us both. I had so many feelings trapped inside, and I couldn't let them out. It felt like I was suffocating. Months went by, and I finally started to break down. I'd go home every day and listen to her problems. Then, I quietly go to my room and start punching myself, pulling my hair, and scratching the skin on my arms. What did I do with all that anger? Well, I found the perfect way; cutting became my best friend. Seeing the blood rise from my wounds was so indulgent and euphoric. It hurt so good. I was starting to function again. Anything bad people were saying about me, my new best friend would fix. My new best friend made me feel so good that I went deeper and deeper each time. My father walked in on me doing my deepest slash. His face took me out of the pleasure; at that moment, the blood wasn't beautiful anymore. It became alarming. I was rushed to the hospital, and some people from P.E.R.T sent me here. So there's my story," she says, letting out a long sigh.

"Nami, I'm so sorry. You didn't deserve any of that! I barely know you, but you've had my back since day one. Your heart is golden, and your loyalty is rare. How dare she take advantage of that? Where is she now?"

"I don't know, probably at home, upset that I'm gone. I'm glad I'm here, away from her. I honestly don't want to go back home. I miss my dad, but I'd rather stay here with you. "I know about cutting."

"Wait, what?" Shock overtakes her face. Showing her my forearms, the scars on my arms become even more visible in the sunlight. Her fingers run along my bumpy flaws.

"Why Sidra?"

"Hiding my pain wasn't smart. It came out in other ways. My thought process for it was that at least I could control this pain. I haven't cut in a few years, but I remember it all too well. I understand what you are going through." Nami rolls up her sleeve, presenting her scabs, surrounded by still-irritated skin. Placing my hand on her suffering, I look into her eyes.

"You can stop Nami. It'll be hard, but I know you can stop. I can help. I know a few tips and tricks. Please promise me that you will try your hardest to stop," I say, raising my pinky finger. Her eyes widen, letting go of a few tears,

"I pinky promise." Our fingers connect.

"I feel relieved that I don't have to hide my arms from you now," Nami says.

"I think you're pretty lucky. You're the only patient who knows about my cutting."

"Wow, I feel special. I wish I could say the same; Felice knows about mine," she says, lying on the grass.

"I'm just glad you shared."

"You are God-sent," Nami whispers.

"What?"

"Nothing, I'll tell you later. I'm kind of overwhelmed with sharing."

"Alright, everyone, group is over!" Finch shouts, jogging the ball back to the bag. Brushing off Nami's back, I pick out the grass blades hiding in her curls.

"I can't wait to come back out here tomorrow," I say, removing the grass from my pants.

"Don't be mad, okay, but I have some bad news."

"Oh?" I ask

"You won't like who is running the next meeting. Let's say the man is evil. No one likes him."

Of course, just when I thought the day would chill out, a new, fresh hell has been introduced. I can't wait to see what this guy is all about.

Chapter Twelve

Wednesday Day, 2

Occasional sniffs and coughs hang in the air. Everyone's mind checks out, leaving a vacant sign in their eyes. Nami's hair covers her face as her head hangs low.

Daric sits in the far right corner of the room, next to the juice boxes. Something is off; by now, Axel or even Talon would have started becoming antsy, wondering when the group would begin. It's like they'd rather wait an hour than have this meeting. Come on, the leader can't be that bad.

Footsteps come from the hall, ripping through the silence. Felice lifts her head just a bit, "Here he comes," she sings softly. Letting out a groan, Axel sits properly on the loveseat.

"Good evening," a full-figured man says, walking in. Silence wanders back into the room as he looks at everyone. Taking a seat, his large bottom presses a few squeaks from the chair. Sighing, the man runs his fingers through his graphite-colored hair.

"Let's get started," The man says, glaring at me.

"I'm Kester. My job is to snap you all back to reality. I pull you out of your heads and give you techniques on ways to defeat depression and anxiety, and the main reason you are all here once and for all. Suicide is never the answer."

"We already know who you are," Axel says, rolling his eyes.

"Great job, Axel, you are always ready to disrespect me. Today, I'm going to need you to shut the hell up. You and I both know there is a new patient in here," Kester says, looking back at me.

"Give me your name."

"Sidra," I mumble.

"Listen, Sidra, you can be one of the few who listen to my wise advice, or you can be like your fellow patients. They will never improve because they would rather have pity parties for the rest of their lives. You choose, what will it be?"

My throat becomes dry as I fidget with my fingers.

"Looks like I know your choice. You will be joining your fellow patients," Kester says with a jagged smile.

"You didn't even give her enough time to answer your stupid question," Talon says.

"Yeah, what Talon said," Daric says from the corner. Talon glares at Daric.

"You all brought this upon yourselves. Don't get upset with me. Instead of seeking professional help from people like me, you decided to make your problems perish with suicide," Kester says.

"Whatever, Dude," Axel says.

"Let's take Felice, for example. Felice, you've been here for a while, but you still never talk in my groups. It must be such a small excuse as to why you ended up here. You don't want help? Do you want me to feel sorry for you?" Kester asks, looking pleased with himself.

"Back off, you don't know what she's been through. She doesn't want to tell you anything because she doesn't like you," Talon says. Felice's breaths become rapid.

"How cute of you to protect her. How can I help her if she doesn't tell me? Come on, Felice, tell us the full story. Why are you here? Is it over a silly breakup with the other patient you met here last time?" Kester says in a mocking tone.

Tears pour from Felice's eyes as she begins to shake.

"Tears aren't going to get you out of this one. I bet the new patient is dying to hear more about you," Kester says. Felice looks at me as her face drowns in tears.

"Stop it, you know nothing!" Felice's voice shakes.

"Then tell me."

"It wasn't over a stupid breakup. I love them both so much! I don't know what happened! My precious baby boy fell asleep next to me. I...I woke up, and he was DEAD!" Felice screams.

She falls to the floor, tears raining from her eyes. "My baby boy is gone because of me! My boyfriend hates me because I killed our son. I'm a murderer!" Felice screams even louder. Getting on my knees, I hug Felice hard. Talon joins me on the floor as she continues to cry and shake.

"Anyone would want to die! I wish my boyfriend had beaten me to death rather than leave me to live without my son! Why did he have to come back and find me strangling myself with a belt? I could have been with my son!" She hollers as snot escapes her nose.

Nami, Axel, and Daric rush to the floor.

"It's okay, please calm down, it's okay," Daric says, rubbing her back.

Talon wipes away the tears on her cheeks.

Kester stands over us, "Get back to your seats now, or I will write you all up!" Kester shouts.

We all hurry back to our seats, leaving Felice on the floor. Felice's legs shake as she stands. She pulls her hood over her face and curls up on the couch.

"You will never know my pain, Kester; no amount of words you memorized in your textbooks will help you," Felice says harshly.

"Yeah, what's your problem? Is this a sick game to you? Yes, of course, we need help and must want it, but this is not the right way to do it. You are pushing us further down the hole!" I shout, my lips tingling with adrenaline.

Kester's face softens for a second and grows hard.

"You may be new, but you will learn to respect me. I can keep you here longer. Watch yourself. Today's meeting is ending early; don't expect this tomorrow," Kester says, glaring at me.

"If you make anyone else cry, it'll be your last day working here," Axel says.

"Keep your empty threats to yourself, little boy. No one will believe anything you tell them about me. I've been working here for years. I'm the best counselor they have." Kester leaves the room.

"Now you know why we don't like this guy," Nami says. Everyone nods in agreement.

"I don't think I can handle more days of this," I say

"I'm just glad he was the last meeting of the day. Are you still meeting Axel at dinner?"

"Damn, I completely forgot. Since this day can't get any worse, I guess I will. If he starts to get all crazy, I'm leaving."

"I'll be there watching. If he tries anything funny, I'll be all over him, ready to throw down."

"Thanks, Nami."

Chapter Thirteen

Wednesday Day, 2

My nails scratch the bottom of my food tray. Anxiety clamps my jaw shut as reality sets in. Maybe I should act like I didn't read the letter and sit down with Nami. Her hand squeezes my shoulder,

"Relax, remember I'll be here if you need me. Just give me a signal, and I'll jump on him if he does anything creepy," she reminds me with a devious grin. I nod, accepting my fate. Axel's eyes grip me as I make my way over to his table tucked away in the back of the cafeteria. Taking a seat, I exhale slowly.

"Hi," squeezes through my clamped teeth. His eyes release me as he stabs at a dark slab of meat crammed between mixed vegetables and lumpy mashed potatoes. Well, this is awkward. Whatever, maybe it's better if we don't talk. Uncovering my dinner, my stomach gurgles as the meat glistens with a mysterious oily layer. Well, that's great, an unappetizing meal with unappetizing company. He shoves one end of the slab into his mouth. His jaw flexes and pops as he rips off a huge chunk. His pink lips shine with the mystery grease as he looks at me with full cheeks.

"You know what, I'm just going to go." Covering my plate, I stand up.

"Please don't," he says with his mouth still full. Sitting back down, I sigh out loud. Unfolding a thin napkin, he spits the chewed-up wad of meat into it.

"This tastes like they boiled this in a vat of oil," he says, trying to wipe the oil from his lips.

"Can we please move on to the reason why you wrote the letter?"

"What? You don't like our little date? You've barely touched your food," he teases.

"Ha, funny. Just spit it out already."

"What's the rush? We both know that we have nothing better to do," he says, pushing his tray aside. Rolling my eyes, I open the small carton of orange juice. Sipping it, I watch as he searches his thoughts.

"So, I'm guessing you're in the foster system?"

"Yeah, unfortunately," he says with an empty expression.

"What do you mean?"

"Come on, Sid, you should know. The adults in the system treat kids horribly. They only see us as paychecks. The more messed up you are, the more they get paid to 'take care of you.' It's disgusting," he explains.

"Yeah, there are some low lives in the system, but they aren't all bad," He chuckles,

"That's a good one. The only reason I'm here is because of my foster parents. They kicked me out the moment I turned 18. You know what that means?!" Confusion overtakes my face. He slams his fist on the table,

"What? You should already know this. When you turn 18, they don't receive any more money for taking care of you. It's all over; the family that you grew up with and that you prayed for to keep you forever casts you aside for a new kid. They don't care where you go. They want you out!"

"I'm sorry, I didn't know that, though."

"Are you kidding me?! You said you're in the system," he says, leaning over the table.

"I was in the system, but I was adopted when I was 9."

Axel's face melts into disappointment.

"Now it makes sense why you stuck up for this garbage system. You were one of the lucky ones who got adopted into their dream family," he mumbles as anger swells in his eyes.

"So, what's it like being a lucky one?"

"Lucky? What are you trying to say? Do you not see where I am right now?"

"You were adopted. Your life is perfect now." Anger thrusts itself up my throat onto my loaded tongue.

"You are an idiot! Just because I was adopted doesn't mean I live in a damn fairy tale. A single woman adopted me. It's just me and her. Even years after the adoption, I still deal with abandonment issues! How's that for your damn fairy tale!?" He opens his mouth, pushing out only a few sounds as his face is consumed with guilt. Sliding my tray aside, I leave the table, stomping my way out of the cafeteria and down the hall.

"Sidra, wait!" Nami calls out. Slowing down, I wait for her to catch up.

"What happened? What did he do?" She asks, out of breath. Covering my face with my hands, tears pour out of my eyes.

"I wish my life were normal. I never asked for any of this! I want to go home!" My chest tightens as my body crumbles to the floor. Nami holds me close to her chest.

"Come on, let's go to our room so you can lie down," She says, trying to stand up with me.

"Can you please leave me alone?" I say, tasting my tears. Her eyes fill with hurt as she lets go of my hands.

"Okay, I'm sorry, I just wanted to help." Seeing the rejection on her face, my heart calls out for her as she walks away.

"I didn't mean it; please come back," I whisper, feeling my sorrow engulf me. Covering my eyes, I let out more tears as footsteps rush past me.

Chapter Fourteen

Wednesday Day, 2

I glance up and down the hall with foggy eyes. Leaning my back against the wall beside my room, I take a deep breath. My dry tears stick to my irritated cheeks as Axel's loud assumptions swirl in my mind.

My heart palpitates as I think about Nami. The way I dismissed her, the only girl my age I've ever met who accepted me the moment she saw me. I wouldn't blame her if she stopped talking to me.

"Deep in thought, huh?" Katrina asks with a warm smile.

I nod as I try to wipe the tear residue from my face.

"Is it okay if I sit here?" She asks, pointing to my side.

Shrugging my shoulders, I slide over a bit. Her knees crackle and pop as she sits next to me. Crossing her short legs, she looks at me with a nurturing look. Chatter from the other patients fills the silence between us.

She clears her throat, "I saw the little fallout you had with Axel. I wanted to make sure you were okay."

"Um, I guess," I say, looking away from her. Her sweet smile and soft eyes confuse me.

I've never seen her look like this before, not even with Axel. Katrina smiles even wider as if she senses my discomfort.

"I know this is different from what you've gotten used to from being here. You know, I'm pretty nice when I'm not working. This job is tough; without armor, my work will bulldoze right through me. You know?"

Nodding, I look back at her face, feeling less discomfort. So this is the real Katrina. It's kind of nice.

"Axel sent me," she says, breaking the silence.

"Great, so I'm in trouble?"

"No, no," she giggles.

Raising an eyebrow, I cock my head to the right.

"He wanted to apologize, but he didn't know how. After you left, he sat there for a minute or so, then ran out of the cafeteria straight to his room. I followed him and saw you in the hall crying," she says, looking at Axel's door.

"Oh. Well, can I ask you something?"

Katrina nods, waiting for me to find the right words.

"How...why do you treat Axel better than us, the other patients?" I ask, feeling out of place.

"That's a long story," she says, leaning her back against the wall. A long sigh slips through her parted lips.

"Okay," I say, facing towards her with wide eyes.

She smiles, "Alright, alright. It was a long day; for some reason, the patients were wild. Something about one of the meeting staff, anyway. It was around the time I normally clock out. Zanna told me that a new patient was coming in, but I told her to let the night staff deal with the check-in. On my way out of the nurse's station, I saw him, and I dropped my things. He didn't look like any other patient I've seen before on the gurney. I wish I could explain the feeling, the presence, I guess you can say, coming off of Axel. I guess the best way to say it was pure agony? I helped the paramedics get him off the gurney. His eyes, the most interesting eyes I've ever seen, locked onto mine. I could tell he didn't trust me, but my armor began to crack. The attitude, the sass, the 'I don't care' were fading before my eyes. It was scary," she says, laughing.

"Then what?" I ask, feeling my confusion and curiosity fade into one.

"I took him into the check-in room. He sat down in the chair, and the whole room felt heavy. He was hesitant to say anything. I was, too; I was worried that my armor wasn't strong enough, that I wasn't ready. Let me tell you, I wasn't ready, but I would do it all over again. I nodded to Axel, and the room flooded with his voice. When he was done, all I could do was hug him. I'm not supposed to get this attached to patients, but I'm only human. Axel needed a human; he needed to know that I had a heart," she says, smiling as she looks up at the ceiling.

Tears begin to build up in my eyes. Axel, what happened to you? My heart aches as my imagination runs with each scenario being offered up.

"What did he tell you?" I ask, wanting more.

'Ah, that you would have to ask Axel. I can't break his confidentiality. I've probably said more than I'm supposed to."

"That's interesting, and I want to know more, but he hurt me tonight. He's not the only one here with issues," I say, feeling bitter.

"I understand, but I think you should give him another chance. He saw something in you that made him want to talk with you about a piece of him."

Looking into Katrina's hopeful eyes, I push aside the argument with Axel.

"Okay, I'll give him another chance," I say with a small smile.

"Thank you, Sidra."

She glances at her watch, "Crap, I have to get back, I'm going to be handing out medication and snacks in a few minutes."

Pulling my knees back to my chest, images of what Axel looked like on the gurney present themselves. What does pure agony look like? Maybe I was too hard on him; what if he's been in the hotter, deeper parts of hell and suffered more than me?

Maybe I have nothing to be angry about. Maybe I'm too soft. Looking up at the ceiling, my muscles tense as memories engraved in my mind come flooding back.

"Snack Time, hurry before I take them home," Katrina yells, bringing me back to the present. Yep, that's the Katrina I'm used to.

Talon starts the line at the window of the nurse's station. Nami steps second in line as the others follow.

Giving a slight wave to Nami, my heart freezes as I wait for any reaction, just a blink. A smile pops up on her worried face as she gives me a small wave back.

Her eyes pull away from mine and focus down the hall. Following her eyes, I turn my head. Axel emerges from his room, walking past me without a word. He joins the line, standing behind Felice.

Looking down, I feel my hope deflate. Maybe Katrina was wrong. He seems more guarded than usual. Looking back at the snack line, I watch everyone grab their snack. Nami jogs over to me, holding a small bag of chips.

"Hey."

"Hi."

Nami begins to laugh.

"What are you laughing at?"

"How awkward this is," she says, continuing to laugh. A smile takes over my face as I begin to laugh as well.

"I'm sorry, Nami. I didn't mean to make it awkward. I was worried you'd be mad at me."

"Why would I be mad at you, silly?" She asks, putting her hand on her hip.

"I was kind of mean when you were just trying to help."

"It's okay, I get like that too. I wanted you to have your space. It's not a big deal," she says, smiling.

"I was being dumb; I overthink a lot," I say, laughing.

She bends over and wraps her long arms around me, "I've got you."

"Ladies, no touching!" Finch yells from the doorway of the nurse's station. We both laugh as she releases me.

"I'm going to finish the movie we're watching. Want to come?" Nami asks, opening her chips.

"I'm going to stay here for a bit more. I'll catch the next movie."

"Okay, if you need me, just holler my name."

Making her way back to the meeting room, Axel passes by Nami with his head down.

Chapter Fifteen

Wednesday Day, 2

"Is this seat taken?" Axel asks with a nervous smile.

Shaking my head, I scoot over. Sitting next to me, he leaves a small space between us. His lips tremble as he opens his mouth. Hesitation holds his tongue in place.

Clearing his throat, his mouth opens again, this time ready with words, "Look, I'm sorry. I guess I never really thought about the aftermath of adoption. I wanted it all to be perfect,"

"I thought it would be perfect, too, until I started having intrusive thoughts of my new mom leaving me. I still have them even though it's been years," I say, looking up at the ceiling.

"That sounds like torture. How do you enjoy your new life when the old one is still hanging on like a leech?"

"Exactly. Even though I was adopted early, I knew what was happening behind closed doors. I was a victim, too," I say, clenching my jaw.

"Damn, I was hoping you missed out on the free trauma. I'm sorry no one was there to protect you."

He leans his back against the wall and closes his eyes. Sighing, he looks at me with a weary smile.

"Did you get a snack yet?"

"No, not yet. I kind of want to stay here, away from everyone else."

"I got you," he says, getting up. He straightens out his hoodie and makes his way down the hall to the snack cart.

Grabbing two bags of chips and two cartons of apple juice, he makes his way back to me.

"Here," he says, placing them into my hands.

"Thank you," I say, tearing open the bag of chips like a wild animal.

"Axel, what happened to you in the system? It's okay if you don't want to talk about it."

"I'll only tell you if you promise you won't tell anyone," he says with serious eyes.

"I pinkie promise," I say, holding my pinkie out to him.

Latching onto my pinkie, his finger tightens. I feel my cheeks grow warm. He smiles as his face begins to turn red.

"Okay, here we go. My mom and dad were drug addicts, and I was taken away from them when I was six," he says, crunching up his chips in the bag.

"That's awful, I'm sorry."

"Yeah, they would oftentimes forget to feed me and constantly would leave me in strange places by myself. Anyways, when I was taken, I was promised by a social worker that I'd be safe in a new home with a new family."

"I was told that too," I cut in.

"Yup, we are all told that, but sometimes it doesn't work out like that. I was placed in a home with five other foster kids. They were all boys. The mom couldn't care less what was happening with all the kids. All she cared about was the paycheck she was receiving for us all each month." Axel's fist clenches as his eyes close.

"It's okay if you want to stop."

"No, it's okay. One of the older boys liked abusing me in every way you can think of. It was hell. But when I look back at it now, I believe he was only doing what was done to him. It still messed me up pretty badly. After that, I was moved around six more times before getting into a good home. At least I thought it was a good home," he says, punching his chips.

"What do you mean?"

"I'll tell you later. I kind of want to stop talking about this."

"Thank you for telling me. I promise no one else will know," I say, reminding him with my pinkie.

"Thanks, Sid."

"Sid?"

"Yeah, short for Sidra," he says, opening his apple juice.

"No one has ever called me that,"

"Good, now I feel special," he says, laughing with a mouth full of chips.

"You know, before I was adopted, I was in eighteen foster homes."

"Damn, that's a lot! So, you get it. I was worried you wouldn't understand. Again, I'm sorry for assuming."

"It's okay, it's behind us now."

"Welp, I'm off to bed. Today was crazy. I'll see you later, Sid," he says, winking at me. Getting up, he grabs his trash and shoves it into his hoodie pocket.

"I'm sorry no one protected you, too."

Tears began to crowd in his eyes. He nods and makes his way down the hall and into his room.

Chapter Sixteen

Thursday, Day 3

"How much do you want to bet this oatmeal has no taste?" Nami says, poking her lumpy oatmeal

"Watch this," I say, taking syrups from yesterday's breakfast. I open three and let them drip into the oatmeal. Taking my spoon, I mix it up well. "Try it," I say, pushing the Styrofoam bowl to her.

She takes a small spoonful and puts it in her mouth.

"That's way better than I thought it would be. I'm going to do that to mine," she says, reaching for a handful of syrup packets.

"Can I sit with you?" Axel asks, standing behind me with his food tray.

"No," Nami says, still squeezing syrup into her oatmeal.

"I wasn't asking you," he says, putting his tray down on the table.

"The answer is still no. Anyone who messes with Sidra has to deal with me," she snaps.

"Me and Sid had a good talk last night. We apologized and everything."

Nami looks over at me with an unsure look on her face.

"You can sit here; it's fine," I say, scooting my tray over.

Taking a seat next to me, he uncovers his breakfast and begins to eat.

"How can you eat it plain like that?" Nami asks with disgust splattered on her face.

He shrugs as he continues to shovel oatmeal into his mouth.

"Guess what, Sidra?" she asks, her smile widening.

"What?"

"I get to see my dad today!" She shouts with excitement

"Really, that's awesome. I remember you mentioning how much you missed him."

"Yep, I'll see him at lunch. Also, I see my psychiatrist today to see if I get to go home tomorrow," she says, dancing a bit in her seat.

I'm happy for Nami, but I'm worried about how her mother will react. I don't want Nami to come back here or worse.

"Yeah, I see my psychiatrist today, too. I think we all see her today. If the meeting goes well, I'll be going home Saturday," he says, wiping his mouth with a napkin.

I hope this psychiatrist is better than the one I have. He never listens to me, especially when I told him my medication wasn't working. He told me, 'Ride it out.' What does that even mean?

"Are you okay? You look nervous," Axel says, examining my face.

"I'm a little nervous to meet with the psychiatrist," I say

"Don't be. She is super nice," Nami says.

"Finish up your last bites. The first group is about to start," Finch shouts.

Throwing away our trash, we make our way into the meeting room. Sitting in our usual seats, we wait for Katrina.

Katrina wheels in her office chair, completing the odd circle. Plopping down on her chair, she manufactures a smile.

"Good morning, everyone."

"Good morning," we all say in unison.

"How's everyone been doing?"

Sighs and mumbling occupy the room

"Okay...I need to ask you all a very important question. It's so we can make your stay at Pleasant Horizons better. Let's get started. If there was one thing you could change about Pleasant Horizons, what would it be?"

"Kester's group," Nami blurts out. Everyone nods in agreement.

"What, why? He's our best counselor," Katrina says with shock on her face.

"Why don't you ask Felice?" Axel says

"Yeah, Kester's meeting was rough," Talon adds.

"What happened, Felice?" Katrina asks, looking concerned.

Felice's eyes widen with fear; shaking her head, she buries her face into her small hands.

"The things Kester said to her were way out of line. I wouldn't want to talk about it either," Talon says, looking over at Felice.

"Can someone tell me what happened? I don't want to sit here guessing," Katrina says, showing off her irritation.

I need to say something, or else Kester will continue to get away with his awful behavior.

"Kester bullied Felice until she broke down crying. He was using her grief against her while he was power-tripping over the rest of us. We tried to help her, but he told us he could extend our stay if we joined in," I say

Katrina's face twists with confusion, "That doesn't sound like Kester at all. He is sweet, genuine, understanding, and is known for going out of his way to help people."

There's no way Kester is like that. He is far from what Katrina described. Was he once like this? I can't see it.

"Maybe y'all need to start watchin' meetins' then since you don't believe us," Daric says bitterly.

"Look, if it happens again, please come get me during the meeting. I need to see it to believe it," Katrina says, crossing her arms over her chest.

The air in the room grows stiff as everyone's hope deflates. How can she not believe us about Kester? This isn't fair.

"Good chat, you guys; Bel should be here in a few minutes," she says, pushing the chair out of the room.

Chapter Seventeen

Thursday, Day 3

Classical music plays as we all focus on our abstract drawings, "Five more minutes, everyone," Bel says, turning down the music. Abstract drawing is more up my alley. I can just let my marker flow without thinking about mistakes. This is so relaxing.

"Be ready to share your thoughts about your drawings," Bel reminds us.

"I'm done," Nami says, folding her paper in half.

"Me too," Daric and Axel chime in.

"Okay, everyone else, stop drawing, please. Who would like to go first?" Bel asks, turning off the radio.

Talon's hand shoots straight into the air.

"Go for it," Bel says with a smile.

"Okay, this is my drawing," Talon holds up a picture of a flower made from various shapes and lines. "I call it life," he says, admiring his work.

"What was the thought process behind life?" Bel asks, getting a closer look.

"Life is full of different types of people and different kinds of stories, and they all come together to create something beautiful and unique. Hearing everyone's reasons for being here gave me a new perspective."

"Amazing Talon, thank you," Bel says, clapping.

"Thank you," he says, looking pleased with himself.

"Who's next?" Bel asks.

"Can I go?" Nami asks

"Sure."

Nami stands up and unfolds her paper. A portrait of a woman without a face, made up of blocks and jagged, shaded pieces, lay on her paper. "Beautiful; what made you draw this, Nami?" Bel asks, leaning toward the drawing

"It's me. I don't know who I am yet, but all I know is that I'm broken," she says, sitting back down. Aw, Nami, my heart aches as I continue to stare at her artwork.

"Thank you for sharing, I know that was tough," Bel says

Daric crumbles up his paper and throws it to the ground. "Why did you do that?" Bel asks, picking up the balled-up artwork.

"Mine sucks."

"Let's take a look at it," she says, uncrumpling the ball. She shows the picture to everyone. Large, thick black lines cover the whole paper. They bend, twist, turn, and collide with each other, creating a space that resembles a black hole of lines and darkness.

"Can you explain what this means?" Bel asks, handing Daric back his picture.

"It's my head. It's what I see in my head every day. It's Angry and scary; sometimes it's all I can see," he says, looking at it.

"Thank you so much for sharing. I think you did an excellent job." Bel says, encouraging us to join in with her praise.

"Felice, how about you go?" Bel asks

"Okay."

Felice holds up her drawing. It's a large, black mass covering most of the paper, with a small, bright yellow circle in the middle.

"This is when I was pregnant with my baby boy," She pushes out.

"How lovely, thank you," Bel says, smiling.

"I guess I'm next," Axel says, showing off his

Different layers of blue with long curves occupy the paper, meeting and connecting at the end to create a wave-like square.

"I think mine is about love, but I don't know why. I just felt it when I was drawing it," he says as his cheeks glow pink.

"Aw, how sweet. Sometimes art is about feeling and expressing, thank you. You're up, Sidra," Bel says.

Raising my art, I show uneven blobs of different muted colors and sizes spread out over the paper.

"Mine is about pain from separation," I say, folding my paper up.

"Wow, excellent work, Sidra. Thank you all for sharing today. I'm so proud. I will see you guys tomorrow for more fun," she says, pushing her cart out of the room.

"Nami, your visitor is here. Everyone else, line up for lunch," Finch says into the meeting room.

Chapter Eighteen

Thursday, Day 3

Situating myself on the old couch, I watch as the others come into the meeting room one by one. Remnants of peanut butter stick to the roof of my mouth. Licking at it, I daydream of the peanut butter jelly sandwich I just ate. That sandwich was the best thing they've served so far. Sinking into the couch, I close my eyes. I wonder how Nami's visit is going.

"Hey Sidra, it's time to meet with your psychiatrist. I'll let Lawton know you won't be attending group," Katrina says, disappearing into the hall as I get up from the sofa.

Walking ahead of me, she takes several turns as I follow behind her, trying to keep up.

"Sidra, I have something to tell you, Katrina says, stopping in the middle of the hall.

"Yeah?"

"I'll be resigning next week," she says, starting to walk again.

"Why, is it something that we did?"

"No, of course not. There is something that I need to do, and my job is getting in the way."

"How does Axel feel about it?"

"I haven't told him yet."

Approaching a black door, Katrina knocks on it several times.

"Come in," a sweet-sounding voice emerges from the other side.

Katrina opens the door, and as I enter the room, I see a large wooden desk and two black, foldable chairs sitting in the middle of the room. A tall, slim, blonde-haired woman sits behind the desk with an inviting smile. Posters of positivity and self-love are sprawled across the white walls.

"Hi Sidra, I'm Dr. Talia. It's very nice to meet you," she says, grabbing a tan folder with my name written on it.

"Hi, nice to meet you too."

"I love your flower clip; it's so sparkly," she says, showing a radiant smile.

"Thank you. My mom got it for me when I was younger."

"That's sweet. Okay, let's see what we have here; it says that you were already taking medication for depression. Did it help at all?" she asks, flipping through several papers.

"They didn't work. I was still super depressed. I tried to tell my psychiatrist back home, but he wouldn't do anything about it. He kept telling me to stay on it and to ride it out," I spill.

"That's very inappropriate of him. He should have listened to your concerns and acted accordingly. I don't understand how some of these people get their jobs," she says, shaking her head.

"I ended up overdosing on my pills because I felt so helpless...and hopeless."

"I'm sorry you had to go through that. Those feelings are scary, and when you feel alone, they intensify, but I want you to know that you aren't alone. You have people who care for you deeply, who will help you if and when you call out," she says, getting up from her chair. Sitting next to me in the other folded chair, she places her hand on my shoulder.

"Do you remember what your medication was called?"

"No, all I know is that they were blue and round."

"That's alright, I'll ask your mother. But I'll be putting you on new medication. You will take it at night because it will make you sleepy. Please let me know if it's not working so I can switch it for you. Remember, you aren't alone; I'm in your corner. Oh, and do me a favor; when you get home, please switch your psychiatrist. You deserve better, Sidra. Feeling relief cascade over my body, I show a big smile. "Thank you so much, I promise," I say, holding up my pinkie finger.

Her pinkie finger wraps around mine, "I haven't made a pinkie promise since I was young," she says, giggling like a schoolgirl.

"Do you know when I will be able to leave?"

"I need to monitor you on your new medication for a few days, then you'll be ready to go, she says, putting away my file. Getting up from the desk, she shakes my hand and gestures at the door, "Thank you for cooperating with me. Remember you aren't alone, she says for a final time. Leaving her office, I feel a spark of hope for the future.

"Looks like you had a good meeting," Katrina says, closing the door behind me. I nod with a smile.

She escorts me to the little park area where the others are playing with a soccer ball. Taking a seat on the freshly cut grass, I look up at the beautiful, clear blue sky. Taking in a deep breath, my muscles relax.

Felice waves in my direction as she makes her way over to me. Shoving her hands in her hoodie pocket, she sits down in front of me.

"Axel wanted me to give you this," she says, handing me a small, folded-up note.

"Thanks." I wonder what this is about. I examine the neatly folded note.

"Are you and Axel a thing?" Felice asks through the sleeve of her hoodie.

"What, no. I mean, Axel is cool and everything, but no..."

"Oh, sorry, I kind of thought because of the note and how you two were talking in the hall last night. You two look cute together," she says, giggling.

Me and Axel together, I let the thought linger in my mind. Axel is cute, but I don't think he even likes me like that.

"What about you and Talon? You two seem super close."

"I wish, but he is going through a messy divorce. I don't want to be in the middle of that. I care for him a lot, but his wife isn't supportive of him. When he lost his job, she called him useless, kicked him out, and threatened to have full custody of his kids." Felice says, scrunching up her face.

"That's so messed up."

"I honestly think he wanted to kill himself because of how she treats him, but Talon is too much of a gentleman to run his wife's name through the dirt. But I don't mind doing it because she is messing with someone that I care about," she says softly.

"How did you and Talon get so close?"

"When I first came here, I was very sick. I was constantly throwing up, and I could barely eat or sleep because I was dealing with the death of my son. It was still so fresh. He was the only one to check on me and to ask if I had eaten. He made sure I stayed warm and cozy when he saw me shivering. This hoodie is his," she says, rubbing the fabric along her cheek.

"Aw, that's so sweet of him to give you his hoodie. I was wondering why it was so big on you."

Mhm, I ended up telling him why I was admitted and what happened. He hugged me tightly and promised me that everything would be all right. We got in trouble big time because we were hugging, but I didn't care; he treated me so well, unlike my boyfriend. My boyfriend was the one who called P.E.R.T. on me. He hasn't called or visited me since I've been here, and I've been here for a while. I'm hoping to get out soon."

"I'm sorry your boyfriend wasn't there to support you in such a hard time. If you need someone to talk to, I'm always here, and of course, you have Talon, too," I say, hugging Felice.

"Ladies, no touching!" Finch says, shoving foam balls into the bag.

"Sorry," we say

"Oh, and Sidra, if you do become a thing with Axel, just be careful. Love inside Pleasant Horizon is different than the outside world. You won't know who they truly are until you are both released," Felice says, brushing the grass off her thighs.

"Gotcha," I say, doing the same.

"Everyone, line up. It's time for your next group." Finch says, dragging the bag of balls to the purple door.

Chapter Nineteen

Thursday, Day 3

Sitting on the sofa, Axel plops down next to me, causing me to sink further into the couch.

"Hey, where's Nami?" I ask

"Katrina said something about her not feeling well. She might be in her room, lying down." Axel says

"Okay, thanks. I'll check on her after this group."

"Did you get my note?"

"Yes."

"Good, read it when you are alone," he says, winking at me. My heart skips a beat as I look into his enchanting eyes.

Collective sighs notify me of Kester's presence. Pushing his squeaky office chair into place, he takes his seat.

"Good afternoon, everyone." Silence lingers

"Where's Nami?"

"She's not feeling well," Axel says

"Of course, she isn't. Just another excuse to ditch my group," he says, almost pouting.

My jaw clenches as I hold my tongue.

"Let's get started. Everyone comes to grab a piece of paper and a pencil. Hurry up, I don't have all day," He snaps, holding out a stack of papers in one hand and a roll of pencils in the other.

Snatching my paper and pencil from him, I retake my seat.

"The word of the day is Selfish. Write that down on your paper. You all have one thing in common, and that is selfishness. Only the selfish want to die," he says with vigor.

"Yo, I'm not selfish," Daric says, rolling his eyes.

"Oh, but yes, you are. If you weren't, you'd be off living your life. Today, we are going to name a few things that we are grateful for. I want to kill your selfishness."

Am I really selfish? I wanted to be free from the pain that others selfishly caused me. I don't know. Maybe I am selfish. Mom said it herself, but maybe that was her anger getting the better of her. Scribbling down, I put two things that I'm grateful for as my mind continues to wrestle with the concept of selfishness.

Axel mumbles under his breath as he stares at his blank sheet of paper.

"Time's up! Sidra, go first," Kester commands.

"I'm grateful for my mom and food," I mutter.

"Are you really grateful for your mother?" Kester asks cocking his head to the left

"Yes, why?"

"That's hard to believe. Why would you attempt suicide if you love her so much? Sounds like selfishness to me," he says, looking proud.

"I love her, but..."

"There are no buts in love," He cuts in.

"That's not fair. You don't know my reasoning for wanting to die. You don't know what I've been through."

"Your choices tell me all I need to know about you."

"Whatever," I grumble

"That's what I thought. Axel, you're next." He says, facing towards him

"I haven't written anything yet," Axel says

"Of course you haven't. Whatever you guys put down will contradict your choices. At the end of the day, your problems aren't bad enough for you to consider suicide."

"Then why ask us to do this?" Daric asks, standing up. Daric's hand balls up into a fist as his face is consumed with anger.

"Sit down. You can't scare me," Kester chuckles.

"My reason for wantin' death is because of my PTSD. You don't know what it's like to live with somethin' so bad. I think I deserve a pass from yo little lesson."

"I don't care if you were beaten by your father or abandoned as a child; there are too many resources out here to get through it all," Kester states.

"Yo, what the hell did you just say to me?" Daric says, lunging at Kester with fire in his eyes

This is getting out of hand. Katrina needs to see this. Jumping up from the couch, I make my way to the door.

Bolting to the doorway, Kester blocks the entrance with his large body. "Think carefully about your next choice, little girl. I can make it to where you'll never leave," he growls.

"Leave her alone," Axel says, getting off the couch.

"What's going on, Kester?" Katrina asks, standing behind him with her arms folded.

"Sidra tried to run out of the meeting room," Kester says, backing away from the doorway.

"I was leaving the room to get you because things were getting heated again."

"I was doing worksheets about gratitude, and Daric and Axel were not cooperating."

"That's not true," Axel chimes in

"Is it true, you guys?" she asks the others in the room. Their heads hang low as silence disperses through the room.

"Come on, you guys, you heard what he was saying to us. Don't let him scare you," I shout.

"That's enough, Sidra. Go to your room. You need to take a breather," Katrina says with disappointment on her face.

"This isn't fair," I say, flinging my balled-up paper to the ground. I stomp out of the meeting room and down the hall. Why are they so scared of him? I don't want to stay here longer, but I also don't want him to keep putting us down. We aren't his footstool.

Entering my room, Nami sits on her bed, quietly facing the wall.

"Hey Nami. You won't believe why I got kicked out of Kester's meeting," I say

Light sniffles come from her direction.

"Nami, are you okay?" I ask, sitting next to her.

"I'm sorry," she whispers.

"What?"

"I'm sorry, I'm sorry, I'm sorry," she says, her voice growing louder.

"What's wrong?"

"I'm sorry I was born. I'm sorry I'm such a burden," she pushes out through clamped teeth.

Turning her towards me, she reveals her arm. Raw, inflamed scratches lay on her pale skin.

No! She isn't a burden, and I'm glad she was born. Why would someone say that about her!?

Taking the handle of a broken fork, she digs the jagged piece into her tender skin. "Stop!" I yell, trying to pry the fork out of her shaking hand.

"Katrina, help!" I scream as hard as I can. Tears flow from Nami's eyes as her face displays pure agony. "Sidra, I'm sorry," she pushes out through heavy breathing. Holding her close, I rock her back and forth.

Footsteps echo up the hall; Katrina swiftly turns into the room. "What's happening?!" She asks.

"Nami is hurting herself!" I cry

"Let me see," Katrina says, viewing Nami's irritated arm.

Glowing bright red, bits of her skin reach into the air.

"Dammit, how did she do this?" Katrina asks, looking for the suspected object.

Opening my hand, I show Katrina the broken fork handle.

"We need to get her to the nurse's station," Katrina says.

Tears start to pour from my eyes as I look at Nami's face again. "Please don't give up, Nami. You've come so far. Don't let this be who you are," I whisper to her.

"Finch!" Katrina hollers.

Appearing in the room almost instantly, Finch stops in his tracks. "Help me carry Nami to the nurse's station," Katrina says, holding her up on one side.

"Got it," Finch says, holding Nami up on the other side.

Watching as they carry Nami out, my heart sinks into my stomach. Where are they taking her? Sitting on my bed, I rub my eyes, trying to get the images of her fresh scratches out of my mind.

Gripping and tapping my arm, I breathe deep, trying to fight the urge I've been battling for years. The same urge that Nami lost to tonight.

Chapter Twenty

Friday, Day 4

Loud voices and sounds of eating fill the cafeteria. Making my way to the table at the far end of the room, I take my seat. I didn't sleep well last night. All I could think about was Nami. I hope she is okay and didn't get into too much trouble for cutting. Waffles and a small bowl of old fruit salad sit on my tray. Anxiety sets in as I look around the cafeteria.

Scanning the cafeteria one more time, I see Nami waving at me from the doorway as Finch hands her a tray. My heart lunges with excitement and relief. Sitting across from me, she places her tray on the table. An insecure smile stretches across her face.

"Are you okay?"

"Yeah," she says, lifting her arm. A large white bandage rests on her forearm.

"What happened?"

"Do I have to talk about it?" She says, chewing on her soggy waffles.

"Yes, you scared me!" I blurt out.

"It's a long story."

"I've got time," I say, raising my eyebrows.

"Fine! So yeah, my mom called during the visit with my dad."

"Oh no."

"Yep, things got pretty bad. She basically told me how much of an accident I was. Then she told me that I was making her look like a bad mother because word got out about me being at Pleasant Horizons.

I held on for as long as I could. I wanted to explode right there in front of my dad, but I didn't want to worry him. When he wasn't looking, I took a fork from my tray and hid it in my bra. I knew it was wrong, but I needed to do it. The pain was building up too much for me to ignore. I broke the fork and blah blah blah.

When they took me away, they put me in this weird room. There was a bed in the middle of the room that had straps hanging from the four corners of the mattress. Three nurses watched me all night, making sure I didn't hurt myself again. The sad part is I have to stay here for three more days because of this whole mess," she says, sighing.

"I'm so sorry she said those things to you. I don't like your mom, but I think it's a good thing you are staying longer"

"Really?" She asks, piercing a syrup packet with her fork.

"Yes, because you don't have to deal with her craziness. You can breathe and be around someone who cares about you."

"True, but how am I going to deal with her once I'm released? I'll end up cutting again," she says.

"Give me your cellphone number before I leave. I'll call you when you need help calming down. You aren't alone anymore."

"Breakfast is over. Please throw away your trash and line up at the door!" Finch interrupts.

"We never had to line up at the door before. I wonder what's happening?" Nami asks, taking her tray to the trash.

"Yeah, this is new to me, too."

Joining the others in a line, Katrina pats down Felice and lets her through the door. Finch does the same to Talon.

"What's going on?" I ask

"Because of last night's little incident, we have to do pat downs to check if anyone is bringing anything out of the cafeteria," Katrina says, patting around my waist and arms. Looking at Nami, her face drops. "This is all my fault."

"It's okay, don't worry about it," I say as Nami gets a more thorough pat down by Katrina.

Letting Nami pass, we make our way into the meeting room.

Katrina follows behind and takes her seat.

"There was an incident that happened yesterday. I'm not going to name names or specify exactly what happened, but as a result, security measures have been heightened. So, this morning, there will be a mandatory room search to make sure no contraband is in your possession," Katrina says

"What? I've never seen them search our rooms before," Felice whispers.

"Everyone, go to your room and sit on your bed and wait until it's your turn to be searched." Nami and I walk down to our room and sit on our beds.

"They're doing all of this because of me. I feel so bad," she says, patting her bandage as she holds back tears.

"Don't cry, it's okay. The search shouldn't take too long, and everyone will probably forget about it later."

"Maybe," she whimpers.

"What if I tell you one of my favorite pieces of advice that helped me stop cutting?"

She nods with excitement.

"I was told a long time ago that when the urge comes up to cut, to grab an ice cube and rub it where you'd normally cut. I ran through a lot of ice cubes, but it helped. The shock of the cold is almost as sharp as pain. It also distracts you the same way pain would." I explain

"That sounds easy to do, I'll try that. Thank you," she says with hope in her eyes.

Finch and Katrina enter the room. "Okay, ladies, stand against the wall." Following his command, we stand on the other side of the room against the wall.

I hope they don't look through my dirty clothes.

Katrina shuffles through my clothes in my cabinet as Finch lifts my mattress. They both drop to the floor, scanning underneath the wooden bed frames.

"All clear. You ladies can wait outside your room while we finish up." Nami and I take a seat outside our room in the hall. We watch as they enter into a few more rooms. "It seems to be going pretty quickly," I say

"Yeah, I think everyone is clean."

"What the hell is this, Axel!" Finch yells out.

"It's none of your damn business," Axel shouts back.

"Katrina," Finch calls her from Felice's room.

Standing in the hall, Finch opens his hand, revealing a wad of tissue.

"This was under Axel's bed," he says, opening the balled-up tissue. Pink, slightly dissolved pills sit in the middle of the tissue.

"He hasn't been taking his medication?" Katrina asks, looking at Axel.

"So, what if I haven't? You know what? Forget this," Axel says, storming out of his room. Finch grabs the back of Axel's shirt, yanking him backward. "Get off me!" Axel shouts, pushing Finch with all his strength. Finch crashes to the floor as shock stretches across his face.

"You little-" Finch bounces up, grabbing both of Axel's arms and placing them behind his back, slamming Axel against the wall with all of his weight.

"Stop, you're hurting him," Katrina yells out.

"Did you not see he put his hands on me? You already know the rules, Katrina. Don't act brand new," Finch says, pressing Axel harder against the wall.

"Let me go! Let me go!" Axel pants as tears slip from his bloodshot eyes. My heart beats slowly as I watch him struggle.

"Please calm down, Axel," I say, walking over towards him.

"Stay back, Sidra," Finch hisses.

"Relax, it's going to be okay," I say, taking a few more steps.

He stops struggling, letting his body go limp. "Good, now keep calm," Katrina says, picking the pills up off the floor.

"Let's go, Axel, you've got a very special evening ahead of you," Finch says, walking Axel down the hall and around a corner.

Nami looks at me with fear in her eyes.

"Where is he taking him?" I ask.

"Maybe they are taking him to the room where they took me."

"Alright, show's over. Everyone, go back to the meeting room now," Katrina barks.

Following Talon, Felice, and Daric, we make our way into the meeting room. Taking our seats, the air fills with whispers and tension.

"What you whispering about?" Daric asks, leaning forward with curiosity.

"Booty Juice," Talon and Felice say in unison.

"Ewe, what's that?" Nami asks with a scrunched-up face.

"It's when they take you into a special room, strap you to a bed, and inject you with something that knocks you out for up to a day," Felice says, mimicking a syringe with her fingers.

"That can't be legal. How do you know about Booty Juice?" I ask

"It happened to my boyfriend when he punched one of the male nurses. After the booty juice, he never started another fight or put his hands on anyone again," she says, nodding.

"Sounds like Daric needs a little Booty Juice, too. Maybe it'll keep his anger under control," Talon says

"Shut up, old man," Daric responds.

I hope Axel is okay. I hope he doesn't have to get Booty Juice. I would be scared to be strapped down to a bed and injected with some unknown substance. Just the thought of it is making me feel sick to my stomach. Getting up from the couch, I approach the nurse's window. Knocking on it hard, Zanna slams the window open.

"I don't feel good. Can I please lie down?" I ask.

"Yeah, whatever," Zanna says, slamming the window in my face.

Making my way to my room, I lay down on my bed as thoughts of Axel crying and struggling to suffocate me. Closing my eyes, I drift off to sleep.

Chapter Twenty-One

Friday, Day 4

"Sidra, honey, wake up."

"Mom?" I ask, half asleep "Sidra."

Waking up, Katrina's soft face greets me.

"How are you feeling?" she asks, sitting on Nami's bed. Sitting up, I rub my dry eyes.

"I feel okay."

"Good. I wanted to tell you that Axel is doing okay. He is going to be asleep for a while."

"Booty juice," I say under my breath.

"Felice must have told you," she says, laughing a bit.

"Yeah"

"Her boyfriend was a handful," Katrina says, looking up at the ceiling with a slight smile.

"How long will he be asleep?"

"Probably until dinner. Axel told me he gave you a note before the whole hallway brawl happened. I think you should read it now."

Nodding, I take the note from my pocket and unfold it. *Dear Sidra, I want to get to know you more. I care for you, and you are unlike any other girl I've met. Please give me a chance to show you more of me. Katrina has promised me something huge, and I want her to tell you what that is; please meet me at the purple door during snack time. I hope to see you there. -Axel*

Looking up from the note, Katrina shows off a warm smile. "Don't tell anyone I'm doing this, okay? I promised Axel at snack time that I'd let you both sit and talk in the small park. I only promised this because I felt bad after telling him that I'd be resigning. You both better be on your best behavior out there. After what he did to Finch, I shouldn't be doing this, but a promise is a promise. I'll meet you both at the purple door when it's time," she says, getting up from Nami's bed.

"Thank you, but aren't you afraid of getting in trouble?" I ask

"Nope, I'll be quitting soon, so there is nothing they can really do if they found out I let a few patients chat in the park area after dark. Oh, by the way, you missed lunch. It's time for Lawton's meeting," she says, handing me a small wrapped sandwich.

"Hurry and eat that before Finch sees you. Then join up with the others in the meeting room." Unwrapping my meal, I watch as Katrina exits my room. Taking huge bites, I inhale the sandwich.

Releasing my legs from the blanket, I stand and stretch my back. Exiting my room, I make my way to the meeting room. Taking my usual seat next to Nami, she smiles at me. "Glad you're feeling better. I was worried about you," she whispers.

Lawton enters the room with his small office chair. Taking a seat, he flashes a smile at us.

"How's everyone doing? Today, we are learning about some very much-needed coping skills. I've been hearing that our emotions have been getting the better of us."

"Why should we?" Daric asks

"When our emotions are out of control, we react poorly, but we can stop them before they grow into something bigger. We are able to process these complex feelings better and make the appropriate choices," Lawton says, passing out papers to everyone.

On the freshly photocopied paper, a long list of coping skills presents itself.

"I'm going to go around the room and ask everyone to read two coping skills that you like from the list. We can start with you, Daric," Lawton says

"Okay, when I'm pissed, I guess I can go for a walk and, um, listen to music."

"What's your favorite type of music, Daric?"

"I like Old-school Hip-hop."

"Very nice. Walking is a great way to process your feelings. Okay, Talon, you're next."

"Wait," Daric blurts out.

"Yes?"

"Do these work on PTSD? Because sometimes all I see is my. . .father, and I can't escape it sometimes, and I freak out," Daric asks with a nervous smile

That must have been what happened the other day when Daric called Talon Dad. Maybe he was in the middle of a flashback or something. I wonder what happened to him to cause him to have to deal with something so horrible.

"Of course, they do; meet me later after group, and I will tell you specific coping skills for PTSD. I'm sorry you have to go through that, Daric," Lawton says with sorrow in his eyes.

Daric nods.

Placing his hand on Daric's shoulder, Lawton turns his attention to Talon, "Okay, Talon, you are next."

"When I'm upset, I will write down my feelings and do meditation," Talon says

"Good, meditation is powerful. It can help regulate your emotions and help reduce stress. Okay, next up is Felice."

"When I'm sad, I will let myself cry, and I'll also punch a pillow," she says

"Letting yourself cry is an excellent choice. Crying cleanses the heart of deep pain. Okay, Nami, you're up."

"When I'm upset, I'll talk to a friend and do deep breathing exercises," she says

"Yes, talking to a friend can help clear out built-up emotions."

"Okay, Sidra, what do you have for us?"

"When I'm down, I'll practice picturing a peaceful, happy place and take a relaxing bath.

"Visualization is such a good one. It can take you from a stressful situation into a beautiful peace of mind. You all did very well today. Please keep the worksheet and refer to it when you need a little reminder on what skills to use when things get a little dicey. That's it for today's group. Talk amongst yourselves until your next meeting," he says, wheeling his chair out of the room.

"You guys, I can't take another meeting with Kester. It's all I can think about. We have to come up with a way to get rid of him or something," I offer.

"There is nothing we can do," Talon says

"Yeah, he holds all the power," Nami adds.

"Will you guys brainstorm outside with me?" They all nod in agreement.

"Line up everyone. It's time for the best group ever," Finch sings while dragging his bag.

We all lineup outside the meeting room.

Chapter Twenty-Two

Friday, Day 4

Huddling up in a small group, we sit in the grass. The sun shines down on my dull skin as a breeze glides across my face.

"Okay, does anyone know about Kester's personal life?"

"No, but I do remember that Felice was saying something about how he had a favorite patient the first time she was here," Talon says

Talon nudges Felice with his elbow. "Her name was Nya, and they were super close." She says, hiding in her hoodie.

"How do we get more information about Nya?" Nami asks.

"Maybe we can break him down?" Talon suggests

"Oh, like bring up the girl Nya," Daric adds in.

"Yes, exactly, but maybe a few of us can share our story like an icebreaker before bringing up Nya," I say

"Ight, I'll do it, but only if you do it first," Daric offers.

"Okay, deal, but we need one more person," I say, looking around the small circle.

Felice nudges Talon. Raising his hand, Talon smirks, "I guess I'll be the third person."

I wish Axel were here to help with all of this. Maybe it's for the best that he isn't here. I don't want him hurting another staff member if things get out of control.

"So, like we break him down with our reasons why we are here, then the final blow will be with Nya?" Nami asks

"Yeah, remember how angry he gets when we bring up our reasons. This could really work, guys," I say with a smile.

"Who wants to deal the final blow to Kester?" Nami asks

"I think Sidra should do it," Felice says

"Yeah," they say in unison.

"Why me?" I ask

"Because you are stronger than us, you aren't scared to speak out against him," Talon says

"I was angry when that happened. I don't know if I can do this, you guys," I say

"It'll be okay. We've got your back," Nami says with a big smile. The others nod in agreement.

Getting up, I stretch out my body. This is going to be hard. I need to share the reason why I'm here and also bring up Nya. I don't want to stay here longer, but it's my last chance to stop Kester from treating us this way. If he genuinely was their best counselor, then I want to bring that back; the other patients deserve it.

"Time for your next meeting!" Finch shouts, getting up from the bench.

"Aw, already?" Talon asks, dusting off his pants.

"Maybe next time you guys should play and enjoy the park instead of chit-chatting for most of it," Finch says, laughing.

Here we go. You got this, Sidra. This is for everyone; they are counting on you.

Lining up with the others, we watch as Finch swings the door open. Following him inside, we gather in the meeting room. Fear engulfs the room as the other's faces show signs of angst.

Kester makes his way into the room and takes a seat. His eyes scan us as a slight smile appears on his thin lips. He loves seeing us like this, scared and quiet.

"Good afternoon," Kester says, still scanning the room.

Come on, Sidra, you can do this.

"Good afternoon," I say back. Kester's eyes dart to mine.

"Hm, today we are going to be doing..."

"I need to say something," I blurt out.

"What is it?" he says through clamped teeth. Everyone's eyes land on me.

Taking a deep breath, I release the fear in my lungs, "I'm adopted. My biological parents didn't want me, so they threw me away; they left me in the foster care system, where I was abused almost daily. I was placed in 18 different homes before being adopted by my wonderful mom.

But recently, my biological mother has been trying to get into contact with me; when she finally did, she called me a bitch for ruining her life. I didn't know how to handle it all. Then I started thinking about if I destroyed my adoptive mother's life, and I began to spiral out of control, leading me to make such a drastic choice that I now regret," I say quickly.

"Wow, no one asked. But since you are being so open, this is your flimsy reason for wanting death?" Kester scoffs

"Yes, because I didn't want to ruin anyone else's life with my presence," I say with force.

Kester's face twitches as he tries to process my words.

Please, Daric, start talking, don't let me face him alone.

Daric jumps off the couch. His mouth opens wide, ready with his story.

"When I was little, my mom and dad didn't have the greatest relationship, but one day, things got really bad; my dad started hurtin' my mom. He hurt her so badly. She was on the floor cryin', and I wanted to protect her. I ran over to her, blockin' his blows from her. He pulled a knife on us, and I tried to wrestle it out of his hands, and he ended up slashin' me on my chest up to my neck. He's in jail now, but every day that I live, it's like he is still around me. His memory will forever haunt me and my mother. I wanted to die because I'm tired of relivin' the same nightmare every day and every night," Daric says, pulling down the collar of his shirt, showing off the whole scar.

"That's enough!" Kester hollers as he stands up. Sweat drips down his brow as anger exposes itself in his eyes.

"Don't say another word! If anyone else speaks, your stay will be extended," he hisses.

Talon takes a deep breath as his lips part.

"I'm sorry you had to go through that," Talon says to Daric.

"That's it! Three more days have been added to your stay, Talon," Kester spits out.

"Welp, since I'm staying here longer, I might as well share my reason for being here." He says, shrugging his large shoulders.

"You better not say another wo-"

"As you all know, I lost my job, but I'm going to be honest with you all. I didn't want to die after losing my job. I wanted to die because I was being verbally abused every day by my wife, who I loved so much. When I lost my job, she became worse. Things started getting physical. I tried to kill myself because I told myself I'd never put my hands on her. It was all too much for me to deal with. I knew I was going to snap on her soon.

Ultimately, it was to protect her and my kids." He says, slumping over in his chair.

"Wow, I was very wrong about you. I'm sorry for saying you hurt your wife and kids. Not everyone is like my father." Daric says with tears in his eyes.

"Everyone, Shut up!" Kester yells.

"It's okay. You've had it bad, and I can see where that anger is coming from now. I'm sorry that I said those things to you," Talon says, standing up.

"Where are you going?" Kester asks

"I'm going to shake his hand," Talon says.

Blocking Talon with his round body, Kester keeps Talon from taking another step. "Sit down."

"Make me," Talon growls.

I need to bring up Nya now before someone gets hurt. Standing up, I squeeze my way in between Talon and Kester.

"What was Nya's story?"

Kester's eyes widen, "How do you know about N-Nya?" he stutters.

"She was your favorite patient, right?" I ask

Darting his eyes at Felice, he groans, "Why is Nya's name being brought up again? You don't know anything."

"I know that you didn't use to be like this," Felice says with her head down.

"What happened to Nya? Maybe we need to call her up and ask her why you've changed," I say, feeling stronger.

"Shut your mouth!" bursts from Kester as a few tears escape from his distraught eyes.

"Why, will she-"

"She's dead!" Kester yells.

The room falls silent as Kester weeps.

"What?" I ask

"She is dead; after being released, she killed herself."

"I'm so sorry-"

"I don't want to hear your sorry. You didn't know her; you don't know how much I cared for her. She left me without even considering staying for me. I'll never forgive her selfish act," Kester says, sobbing.

My jaw clenches as I search for soothing words to say

"She had the worst childhood. Everyone was so surprised that she was still alive after all the crap she went through. She confided in me and trusted me. Why would she do that and then leave me here holding the broken pieces of what used to be her?" Kester says, dropping down into his chair. His large hands cover his face.

Talon places his hand on Kester's back. Wrapping my arms around Kester, I hug him tightly. Everyone follows as they hug and comfort Kester.

"I may not have known her, but she was special to you, and that's all that matters. I'm sorry for your loss," I say

He lost someone so special to him that he made sure he guarded his heart from it ever happening again. He is not over Nya's death and won't be for a long time.

Letting go of Kester, I remove his hands from his face, "Maybe you need to take a break from this line of work until you can grieve Nya properly." I suggest looking him in his eyes.

"I think so too, but I love this job; I can't see myself doing anything else," Kester says, using his forearm to wipe away his tears.

"But your pain is getting in the way of your job. You're hurting patients and not helping like you used to. Nya would be disappointed if she saw the way you were treating your patients," I say

"You're right. I'm going to take a break. I'm sorry, everyone, for how I've been behaving. I'm so scared of getting attached and losing you guys. I care for you all, even Axel," he says between sniffles.

"I hope you get better soon," I say.

"Thank you, Sidra. That's the end of group today," he says releasing himself from the group hug. Pushing his chair out of the room, he waves goodbye to us.

Letting the air in my lungs out, I breathe deeply. "That was not how I thought the plan would go."

"Same," Felice and Talon say at the same time.

Nami wraps her arms around me, "You did so good!"

"I feel really bad for him; I hope he gets the help he needs," I say, wiping away a stray tear.

"It's time for dinner, everyone," Katrina shouts into the meeting room.

The air feels lighter than ever before.

Chapter Twenty-Three

Friday, Day 4

Turning the corner, I see Axel and Katrina waiting for me at the purple door.

"About time," Katrina says, unlocking the door quietly.

She hands us both a snack and a juice box and pushes us out the door. Katrina makes her way to the bench and sits down with an old book in hand.

Taking our seats, we sit on the damp grass. The cold night air nips at my cheeks as the moon glows over our heads. Tall lamp posts illuminate our smiling faces.

"Want to hear something cool?" Axel asks while opening his snack.

"Sure."

"You're leaving tomorrow morning," he says

"Really? How do you know that?"

"I heard the nurses talking about you and some others while I was waking up." He says, chewing loudly on his chips.

I'm glad that I get to go home tomorrow. I love the people in this place, but I miss my bed, my mom, and decent food. It's been a crazy four days here.

"How are you feeling after the…"

"The what?" He asks with wide eyes

"The booty juice," I whisper.

"Gross, what's that?"

"It's when they inject you in the butt, and it makes you go to sleep for a long time," I say, sipping my juice.

"Oh. Yeah, the shot hurt, but I was out like a light before I could complain. I didn't know they called it booty juice. That's a weird name."

"It is," I say, laughing.

"I wanted to tell you how I ended up here. No one knows the full story except for Katrina."

Scooting closer to Axel, I give my full attention to him.

"Remember how I told you I finally landed in a good home? It was a good home all the way until my 18th birthday. I came home from school and saw all my stuff packed on the front lawn. There was a note that said, 'Happy Birthday, we love you.' I went into the house confused, and neither one of them would look at me. So, I start shouting to get their attention. My foster dad finally started to talk, and he told me it was time for me to move on. I got so mad and started shouting even more, then everyone was screaming. It got so loud, and I got so angry that I punched my foster dad right in the face. Then we got into a huge fight. He punched me several times in the stomach and face, and I got him a few more times in his face and body. It was bad. He yelled that I wasn't his kid and that he didn't give a damn where I went. That hurt. It hurt almost as much as not seeing my real parents again. So, I ran up to the roof because I was done with not being wanted. I was going to jump. My foster mom called the police, and they talked me down and took me in, and that's how I ended up here."

"Wow. I'm so sorry," I say, placing my hand on his thigh.

"I believed in my heart that they loved me and I was their kid even though I wasn't by blood," he says with tears lingering in his eyes.

My heart aches as I look into his magnificent eyes, "Just because they couldn't see the amazing person they had doesn't mean other people won't appreciate you."

"I can say the same for you," he says, leaning closer to me.

"I ruin lives."

"No, you don't. Please get that out of your head. I think you've made everyone's life here a little better. Nami was gushing about how you executed your plan for Kester so that he could stop treating us like trash. I heard about how strong you were and how you didn't back down even when it got hard.

You think of others and not just yourself. You have a big heart, and that's what I like about you," he says, gripping my arms.

"Thank you," I say, trying to hide my blushing cheeks

"No, thank you for being your beautiful self. I'd probably be in way more trouble right now if you didn't calm me down in the hallway."

"I didn't want to see you hurt because I... I care about you, too." I say, feeling my heart thump with elation

He leans closer to my face; our lips lightly touch. My heart stammers as my face grows warm with excitement.

"Hey, you two, I thought I told you to behave," Katrina says, putting her book down.

Pulling away from each other, we smile. Axel winks at me as he gets up from the ground. "Will you want to see me once I'm out of this dump?"

"Yes, as Nami would say, Duh!" I say giggling

"I have something to tell you, Axel," Katrina says

"Yeah?"

"Once you are released, you'll have a place to go."

"Really!? Where?" Axel asks, jumping with excitement.

"You'll be staying with me as long as you need," she says with a warm smile.

"Thank you so much, Katrina! Now, it all makes sense as to why you are resigning. I'm the luckiest dude," he says, wrapping his arms around her waist.

"You better not tell anyone until my job here is done,"

"Gotcha," Axel says with a huge smile.

"I'm so glad you have somewhere to go."

"When are you leaving?"

"I don't know. I know it's not anytime soon after what I did to Finch,"

"Yeah, you did a number on him. Alright, you two, it's time to get to bed. Go ahead and hug really quick. I know you want to," Katrina says, smiling.

Wrapping my arms around Axel, our bodies press together, creating a warm sensation. Pulling away from each other, he winks at me.

Sneaking back into my room, I crawl into bed. Snuggling under the sheets, I think of Axel's warm lips against mine. Butterflies tumble around in my stomach as I drift to sleep.

Chapter Twenty-Four

Saturday, Day 5

"I can't believe you are leaving me. I'm going to miss you so much," Nami whines.

"I'm going to miss you too," I say, holding Nami's hand under the table.

"Here, take this," Nami says, handing me a piece of ripped paper.

"What's this?"

"It's my cellphone number."

"Okay, when I get home, I'll call it. I'll leave you a voicemail, and it will be waiting for you when you get home."

"I can't wait to hear it," Nami says, smiling.

"Hey, Sid," Axel says, sitting next to me with his tray.

"Hey," I say, blushing.

"Here's my number," he says, handing me a small folded piece of paper.

"What's the first thing you are going to do when you get out?" Nami asks, playing with her dry pieces of cereal

"I'm going to take a bubble bath," I say, laughing.

"I'm going to miss you. Don't forget about us," Axel says

"I could never forget you guys."

"Sidra, please come to the nurse's station," Katrina shouts across the cafeteria.

"Looks like it's time, guys," I say, getting up from the table

"No," Nami says, grabbing onto my arm.

"It's going to be okay. You'll be out soon, and we can see each other again."

Letting go of my arm, Nami sits back down with tears in her eyes.

"I'll come with you to the nurse's station. I need to take my medication," Axel says, getting up.

We make our way to the nurse station window. "Wait here while I get your stuff," Finch says

I watch as Axel knocks back his morning pills.

"Here is your duffle bag; let's go to your room to pack your things," Finch says, handing me my bag.

Entering my room, I begin to ball up and throw all my clothes into the duffle bag. Finch pulls out my laces for my shoes from a plastic baggie.

"Go ahead and lace up your shoes. I don't want you tripping and hurting yourself when you're out there," he says with a little laugh.

Lacing up my shoes, I think of seeing my mom again. Excitement courses through my body as I put on my shoes.

"Ready?"

Nodding yes, I zip up my duffle bag.

"Good, your mom should be here now." Walking out of my room, Daric, Talon, and Felice all wave at me from the nurse's station.

"Bye!" they all shout.

"Thank you for everything," Talon hollers

"Don't forget us!" Daric shouts

"I won't," I yell back.

Nami and Axel run down the hall to me, both of them hugging me tightly.

"Aww, I'll let this one slide," Finch says with a smile.

"I'll call you both; I pinkie promise," I say, holding out my pinkie. Our pinkies wrap around one another.

"Let's go. We don't want your mom waiting too long. I know she wants to see you, too," Finch says, pulling me away.

Walking down the hall, we make several turns. The butterflies and flowers greet me again on the walls. We approach a big, heavy door. Reaching for his keys, he unlocks the door.

"Sidra!" My mom opens her arms wide, greeting me with a soft smile.

Running into her warm embrace, I drop my bag on the ground.

"I've missed you so much," she says, holding back tears.

"I'm so sorry, Mom. I'm sorry for everything. Are you still mad at me?"

"It's okay, honey, and of course not. I'm glad to see that you are doing better."

"I have so much to tell you."

"You can tell me everything on the car ride home. We can stop at your favorite restaurant and grab a bite to eat, too."

"We get to go to Forked Up?!" I squeal

"Yep, it'll be a nice welcome-back meal. We can talk about anything and everything you want."

"When will I get to see Bevan?"

"He wanted me to tell you that he has the day off tomorrow and that he'd love to meet you over smoothies."

"That sounds awesome. I can't wait to tell him everything."

Waving at Finch, he closes the door with a smile.

The sun shines on my skin, warming my body and energizing it. The wind pushes my hair around my face as the birds chirp, flying through the clear blue sky.

It feels good to be out. Looking back at the door, I smile; I'll never forget what happened.

About the Author

171

Stephanie Christian is a passionate storyteller with a heart for exploring raw emotions, complex characters, and the quiet strength found in life's most challenging moments. When she's not writing, she enjoys gaming with her friends, writing short stories, and getting lost in the stories of others. *Paralyzed Hope* is her latest self-published work, inspired by the resilience of hope even in the darkest times.